A
LEGACY
OF
DARKNESS

ISBN 978-1-7378806-0-8

A
LEGACY
OF
DARKNESS

J.M. WALLACE

To the readers who feel that one adventure is never enough.

THE BEYOND
Druid
Tribe
Blight
Ravenwood
Ceasy Lagoon
EASTERN
ISLES
NORTH
ASTERION
Norbrach
Living
Sea
ummer
Palace
SAGON
Blight
Patsu Trade Route
Patsu
Trade
Harbour
Spreading
UTH
RION

ASTERION MAGIC SYSTEM

Magi – Those born with the ability to wield magic.

Sorcerer
The highest order of Magi, trained extensively in the arts of alchemy, enchantments, and incantations. Their magic is driven by invention rather than nature.

Mage
Ranked under Sorcerer, these Magi are still undergoing training to rise to Sorcerer. Some are not powerful enough to advance to the next level.

Druid

The first Magi, an ancient people who once wielded powerful magic gifted by The Mother herself. Their magic is derived directly from the land, tying them directly to nature and the divine.

Witch

A lower caste of Magi, deriving their magic from herbs and concoctions. These Magi are rumored to be distant descendants of the Druids, resulting in magic more reliant on nature and the divine.

Ancient creatures and Forest Dwellers

Less powerful Magi with ties to the land. They do not rely heavily on their magic, but rather their *connection* with nature.

Nefari

Dark Magi who derive their power through sacrificial magic. They are dangerously powerful, but at a great cost. These Magi are outlaws in both human and Magi society.

CHAPTER ONE

Shaye, Twelve Years Ago

It was *Shaye's favorite time of year;* and tonight, King Idor was pulling out all the finery for the grandest ball they had seen yet. Shaye looked up in awe at the beautifully decorated hall, which was aglow with enchanted candles hovering in the air above the bustling ballroom. The golden light danced off the white stone walls, as if the candles themselves were performing a waltz just for her. Around the room servants prepared for Asterion's biggest event of the season; the Winter Solstice.

The smell of sweetbread filled the air, warm and inviting. Shaye's mouth watered and she wondered if she could sneak some away before the big event; sometimes the cooks would leave them out for her to swipe when Nanny Jin wasn't looking. She crept unnoticed through the ballroom past a group of Sorcerers and the Mages who were apprenticed to them. She moved quietly, glad they were too distracted with the task of enchanting ice statues in the shapes of various magical creatures from the Raven Wood to notice a mischievous ten-year-old girl. Shaye giggled as she saw the sculptures crack under the apprentices' fruitless efforts to spell them into movement.

She was nearly to the servants' entrance, headed for the kitchens. The smell of her favorite treat was growing stronger, mixed with the delicious scents of lamb seasoned with fresh rosemary from the gardens. Footsteps interrupted her thieving plans, and she ducked behind the nearest pillar. Grace was not a quality Shaye possessed, so it was no surprise when she tripped over her own two feet right into a nearby potted fern. Dirt spilled over onto her brand-new Winter Solstice gown. Shaye blew a loose strand of her chestnut brown hair from her face and desperately tried to wipe the mess from her expensive dress, knowing her aunt was going to be furious with her. A few Sorcerers looked toward the commotion, but Shaye knew they could not be bothered with childish Magi running wild in the castle; they went back to their enchantments, ignoring her as usual.

Suddenly someone grabbed her shoulders from behind, making her topple backwards into a tall, thin body. She looked back into the wide grin of a shaggy, dark-haired boy: Bastian. She was delighted to see her best and only friend. He was the only person in the palace who accepted her for who she was, and she adored him for it. He did not mind that there were always bruises on her legs from climbing trees in the Raven Wood, or that she always ate one or two more sweet rolls at dinner than she should, unlike the other children residing in the palace, who believed they were better than an orphaned Druid girl who had not yet mastered her magic.

She turned her attention back to Bastian, who was already dressed for the ball in a fine suit his father had commissioned for him. He looked like the dark prince from a fairytale, dressed in all black with an obsidian stone hanging from a leather cord around his neck. She blushed when he caught her staring.

He smiled wickedly at her. "You missed your enchantment lessons again today."

She gave him her best impression of pure innocence, "I got lost."

Bastian scoffed at the sorry lie. "Your absence draws unwanted attention from the Master Mages."

The Master Mages, who had the unfortunate task of training the young, unruly Magi in the palace, held a particular distain for her. She sighed, "Failing at every incantation I attempt draws even more unwanted attention. So, what's the point?"

Bastian nudged her in the shoulder playfully, "Don't worry, I covered for you. You owe me though, I had to partner with Liana. All she could talk about was the new dress her mother had gotten her for this ridiculous ball."

Shaye was grateful to Bastian for covering for her; it was something she had been making him do more and more over the last few weeks. Bastian was advanced in his studies and respected because of his family's name, while hers was of an ancient bloodline of less powerful Magi. Unless she was working with elemental spells, she struggled in her studies, and the Master Mages thought her lazy for it.

Bass took her hand. "Hurry, Shaye, before my father catches us here. If he does, he'll make us practice incantations until the party." They giggled as they ran through the servants' door and to the King's dining room. The room provided the cover they needed with everyone else busy setting up in the ballroom. "Where are we going, Bass?" she asked, though it did not matter to her. She would follow him anywhere.

He hushed her as a frightening man in an ugly green cloak strode into the room: it was Bastian's father, Baal. Shaye had been terrified of the man since the first moment she saw him. There was something sinister about him, the way his face was all sharp angles and high cheekbones. She could not remember ever seeing the man smile, not even toward his own son.

Bastian had come to live at the palace four years ago, with his father who was to be the new Magi advisor to the King and the highest ranked Sorcerer in Asterion. Baal worked closely with her uncle, doing the King's bidding, which meant Shaye had to spend more time around him than she would have liked.

She tugged on Bastian's sleeve. "Let's get out of here."

Bastian ignored her, holding out his hands and mumbling something under his breath; though she could not see it, she could feel his magic forming around them. He shielded them both with his magic, blocking sight and sound from his father and the man who had just joined him.

"Bastian, we shouldn't be here."

"Shh, I want to listen."

Shaye crouched down next to him with a huff of annoyance and watched the two men. The second, who had joined Bastian's father, was a man she recognized from her uncle's meetings: Lord Brayham. He was a man with a mean streak, and she had seen it often in the way he treated the servants and even his own wife. Shaye had once seen him pinch his wife in the arm when she spoke out of turn at a dinner they'd had with an ambassador from Sagon. It was no wonder his daughter was such a terror. Duchess Adella had taken to calling Shaye names and teased her for being a Magi who could not access her magic easily, not that Adella had any powers of her own, having been born mortal.

Baal and Lord Brayham were arguing in a hushed tone, and it was difficult to hear them through Bastian's shield. Baal grabbed Lord Brayham by the collar. "Do not test me. The things I can do to you, to your family, will make you *beg* me to end you all."

Lord Brayham trembled, but still he said, "You Magi think

you're untouchable. I may be mortal but I am not without friends and power. Careful, or you will find yourself subjected to *my* mercy." He pulled away, smoothing out his shirt over his large belly.

Bastian's father warned him once more, "Leave it alone, Brayham. You do not want to find yourself on the wrong side of this." He stormed out before a shaken Lord Brayham did the same.

Bastian lowered the shield once they heard their footsteps retreating down the hall. Bass was silent, so Shaye nudged him. "Can we go now? I want to sneak through the kitchens on the way out." She pulled on his hand, leading him away from the dimly lit room.

Reluctantly he followed through the kitchen where Shaye snagged two rolls, one for each of them. The two of them made their way out the back door to the stable yard outside. Shaye shivered from the cold and held a roll out to Bastian. Before he took the roll from her hand he grabbed her arm, suddenly sounding urgent, "Shaye, whatever you do, make sure you stay with me tonight at the ball."

"Of course." She had a mouthful of the sweetbread, savoring it. "Who else would I stay with? Anyway, you have to help me avoid that pinch-faced Adella," she teased with a wrinkle of her nose. "She was telling everyone about the dress her mother had imported from-"

Bastian shook her, "Shaye, *focus*. You need to stay with me. I have been hearing things; my father isn't acting like it, but he's scared." Bastian's warm, chocolate brown eyes bore into hers. "Please, promise me that you won't leave my side."

Shaye nodded seriously, crossing an *X* over her heart. "I promise, Bass."

That seemed to make him feel better, so she took the opportunity to lighten the mood. She grinned, taking hold of his leg and with a swift pull he was on the snowy ground. He yelped out with laughter, already pushing himself up. He raised his hand and there was a faint shimmer in the sunlight as he whispered the words, "Ow-ft-ir." The soft sunlight shimmered at his call, and a snowy drift swept up and into the air, flying around her in glittering tendrils. She giggled as the cool flakes tickled her neck and mussed her neatly brushed hair.

The two of them took off in a race, running toward the sparkling lake where the winter ice was beginning to form. The cold did not slow her down as she and Bastian fled the party preparations.

Years from now she would look back on this moment. The joy and safety she felt, rosy-cheeked and giggling with her closest friend. Listening to the icicles chime in the trees. The sight of the white stone palace reflecting on Brenmar Lake. And the distant sound of people greeting one another as they climbed from their gilded carriages in all their finery.

It was the last moment in which she had felt truly safe and at peace. Before she went back into that magnificent ballroom. Before the chaos began and she was separated from Bastian. Before she was left with the memory of the screams and the scent of terror that would haunt her dreams for the rest of her life. Before the magic was gone.

CHAPTER TWO

S orin sat at his father's bedside, close enough to touch the pale-faced man lying there soundlessly. His father, King Allerick, had been like this for days now. What had started out as a cold, turned quickly into a full-fledged attack on his body.

Attendants and doctors had been bustling in and out of the room all day, ignoring Sorin completely. Not that it bothered him, he was here out of concern; and if he was being honest, he was also there out of guilt for the argument they'd had when his father had last been well enough to speak.

Sorin leaned forward in his seat, looking down at the man who had always seemed larger than life. Sorin rubbed his temples in a fruitless attempt to rid himself of the headache that had presented itself hours ago. The past haunted him often, but today the memories were relentless. It had been nearly twelve years since the glittering winter night when his father had swept into a beautiful golden ballroom and spilled blood on the freshly polished marble floors; before taking the crown from King Idor.

Now his father was on his sickbed and Sorin was forced to wait as helpless as he had been in that ballroom when he was a young boy. He shifted uncomfortably in the seat he had taken up beside his father's bed; his long legs felt restless from sitting so long. He ran a hand through his neatly trimmed, sandy blonde hair and thought about how quickly a person's position in life can change. He had gone from nothing more than a distant cousin, of a line forgotten, to heir of the throne, with a slash of his father's sword.

Glass shattered on the floor, bringing Sorin's attention back to the dimly lit room. It startled him, but his father remained in a deep slumber. Nothing was able to stir him to consciousness over the last couple of days.

The apologetic attendant, who had dropped the glass, bowed to Sorin and his father. "Apologies, your Royal Highness." He began sweeping up the fallen glass.

"No need for apologies." Sorin gave the flustered man a reassuring smile. "Is the doctor back yet?"

"He is on his way now." The attendant frowned. "Has there been any change?"

Sorin shook his head, and the man gave him a sympathetic smile before excusing himself from the room. Sorin closed his eyes again to get some more rest, but visions of the coup still danced in his mind. He had always struggled with how his father had taken the throne; and even now in his chambers, with his father on his sickbed, Sorin could feel that seed of resentment. He shook his head trying to rid himself of the memories and was grateful when his father's secretary interrupted them.

"Apologies, Your Highness, but I have some papers here that need to be signed." The frail man shifted uncomfortably. Gendry, who was not much older than Sorin, had always been a nervous man.

"I do wish people would stop apologizing to me today."

Sorin chuckled, taking the papers reluctantly. The last thing he wanted was to deal with matters of state.

"It is just a few documents regarding the Guilds... There are funds that need to be authorized and disbursed."

The Guilds were his father's pride and joy, and one of the first things he had enacted as the new ruler of Asterion. Sorin sifted through the papers. The Guilds were created after King Idor's overthrow to give power to the people that had been neglected and abused under his rule. They were made up of tradesmen, masons, and the like. It was one of the many improvements that his father had made throughout the kingdom.

Sorin began skimming through the documents half-heartedly, signing the papers he knew his father would approve. It was impressive, really, the work that his father and his supporters had done. As bitter as Sorin was about the violence he had witnessed on the night of the Winter Solstice, he was in awe of his father's determination. Throughout the rebellion and his time as the new king, he had never wavered in his beliefs.

Gendry lingered nearby, waiting for the documents to be ready for him to deliver into town. Sorin called to him when he came across an alarming piece of paper. It was an arrest order for a Magi in the harbour. Sorin called to the mousey man, "Excuse me, what is this?"

Gendry approached to get a better look at the warrant. "Ah, yes, that... A Magi man was reported to have been performing magic."

"Blood magic, you mean." Sorin read over the document again. Magic had not been successfully performed in Asterion since Idor's overthrow. It was, in fact, impossible to use. His father had made sure of that, banishing magic throughout the kingdom with a powerful relic from The Beyond; a treacherous land that no mortal had dared venture into for centuries. It was ultimately what had made his father a man of legends.

Sorin did not know much of the relic, only that it had immense power granted from The Mother of creation, herself. His father had found a way to activate it so that the only magic that could be accessed in Asterion was dark, blood magic, something the relic had proven unable to banish. That sort of sacrificial magic was punishable by death. If Sorin signed this paper now, it would be a death sentence for the Magi in question.

He shook his head at the secretary. "I cannot sign this."

The man's eyes shifted toward Sorin's father, unconscious from the sickness that was raging inside of his body. Sorin knew Gendry did not want to argue with the crowned prince, but he, like Sorin, was a mortal; meaning that he likely held the same prejudices against Magi as most of the other mortals in Asterion. Under King Idor's rule, the most powerful Magi had risen high in status and had abused that power. While the people of Asterion had struggled to feed their families, Sorcerers and Mages enjoyed the comforts of court alongside the careless aristocrats.

Sorin sighed, "I will have my men investigate the matter further. We need to have substantial evidence of wrongdoing before making an arrest." Sorin would feel more confident having his own men look into the matter. Accusations like this were common in Asterion. Often, they were a result of prejudices the mortals held toward their Magi neighbors.

Gendry relaxed his shoulders. "Yes, of course, Your Highness."

Sorin handed Gendry the stack of papers and the man bowed, ready to take his leave. Sorin stopped him before he made it to the door. "Your family... You lost them to the old king's Sorcerers?"

When Gendry turned to him there were tears in his eyes.

"Yes, Your Highness. One of the old king's Sorcerers came to our farm and set our home on fire."

Growing up, Sorin had heard stories like this while sitting in on his father's secret meetings. The things King Idor's Magi had done to mortals throughout Asterion were horrific. Men who attended these meetings would give depositions about these occurrences. The terror of these accounts ranged from a Sorcerer of King Idor's court casting spells on mortal men, making them choke on their own blood, to a Mage who snapped a servant's neck for not filling his glass to the brim.

Sorin recalled a haunting report about a farm that had been torched by one of King Idor's Sorcerers. Only the Sorcerer hadn't just set fire to their farm... He had drowned the men's children by pulling water from their well and engulfing them in it. Sorin's heart ached for the man standing before him, and now he understood why Gendry would crave justice against any Magi rumored to be using magic, even after all these years.

Sorin's stomach twisted into knots. "But he spared you?"

"Yes." Gendry wiped his tears away and set his jaw. "He said that I was weak, and he did not feel like wasting any more of his energy on such meaningless creatures."

Anger boiled in Sorin's veins. He wanted to make up for the pain that this man had endured and was tempted for a moment to sign the warrant after all. Sorin shifted in his seat, but before he could say anything, the palace doctor interrupted.

Gendry excused himself, and Sorin turned his attention back to his father. The doctor busied himself in the corner of the room, far enough away that he could not hear Sorin. Sorin leaned closer to his father and took his hand.

It was cold, so Sorin rearranged the blankets so that his father would be better covered. His father did not stir and Sorin sighed before speaking to him, "I know what you would say... I should have signed the warrant." His father continued to sleep peacefully as Sorin continued, "I just..." Sorin's voice broke. "I'm sorry, father. I'm sorry that I'm not more like you. I'm sorry that we have had trouble seeing eye to eye, but it doesn't mean that I don't respect the kind of man you are..." At Sorin's words, his father's eyes fluttered, but did not open.

Sorin shouted for the doctor, "I think he's waking up!" It had been days since his father had stirred, and the doctor came running. His father's eyes stilled again, and the doctor put his fingers on Sorin's father's neck to check his pulse. The doctor furrowed his brow and shook his head. The look on the doctor's face told Sorin, once again, his life had changed in the blink of an eye. His father, King Allerick, was dead.

A ringing filled Sorin's ears as he fought back the tears threatening to fall from his dark blue eyes; the doctor scurried to a guard by the door, and before Sorin knew it, he was swept up in a sea of courtiers. Noblemen, guards, and councilmen shoved their way into the generous quarters of the King. Sorin's head was swimming, and he was certain he was about to be sick on the exotic, imported rug his father had gotten from a smuggler in the Padsu Harbour. He focused on that rug, and the intricate pattern that swirled into the form of a sea dragon, as people in the room cried out in grief.

"Enough." A commanding voice cut through the room with unwavering authority. Queen Evelyn, his mother, stood in the doorway of the King's chamber. *Late king,* Sorin had to remind himself. Despair was creeping in quickly.

The room went still and silent as every courtier turned to bow. His mother stood before the court, tall and regal in a deep blue velvet gown. It was a simple dress, as was their court's style, but elegant, nonetheless. A life in the sunshine marked itself on her face in the small lines that came with age. Her blonde hair was swept back and topped with a jeweled crown. It was the only adornment she ever wore.

Seeing her standing there, it was hard for Sorin to remember the shy, soft-spoken woman she had been before the uprising.

She came to Sorin's side, embracing him with a warm hug. Then she turned to her late husband, kneeling at his bedside. A hush fell over the crowd as she took his hands in hers and kissed them sweetly. Sorin stood in a daze. He wanted to reach out to his mother, but couldn't bring himself to move. All he could do was think of the many things that he had wanted to say to his father, but now it was too late.

After a few moments, his mother stood again. She smoothed out her dress and wiped the tears that were streaming down her face. Sorin knew she was holding in the immense pain she was feeling; just as he would now be expected to do. They would need to present themselves with strength and dignity; forced to grieve properly in private.

Worrying about appearances was something that Sorin had always struggled with, and this was no exception. Before the coup, neither of Sorin's parents had been comfortable at court. They had not agreed with the prestige the Magi held there under Idor's rule, while the common man struggled for any semblance of power and respect. But they had believed in their duty to the people of Asterion... It was one of the many things that made them a perfect match.

Sorin, on the other hand, had never quite adjusted as princeling, and though it had taken time for his mother to adjust, she had persevered; assuming the role the people needed in uncertain times such as this. The regal woman who stood before him now was not the same merchant's daughter who had read to him in the garden or taken him to the fish market every Sunday. Years as queen had made her stronger; a steady power illuminating from her in any situation. The court now welcomed her presence as if they would become stronger just by being near her.

Her voice echoed in the large room as she continued, "The

King is dead. Long live his heir, King Sorin." She gestured to Sorin, and the court turned all eyes on him. Sorin's heart lurched in his chest at the sound of the title before his name. As the courtiers bowed to him, there was a mix of grief, panic, and envy on their faces.

Sorin knew they were wary of what would happen with him ascending to the throne in his father's place. He had always conducted his duties as prince by the book. He'd attended countless tiresome council meetings, studied the art of leadership and philosophy, and pored over the histories of Asterion and even Magi. But he had not proven himself yet. His father had risen to king and had inspired the people to keep him there. He had made them feel safe and empowered, and had cast out those who had taken from them, oppressed them, and threatened them. He had outlawed magic to level the playing field for those who had been born without it. And he had done it all through sheer will and determination.

Since then, there had been the occasional dispute in the villages. Though many Magi fled after the uprising, the ones who had remained faced attacks in retribution of old grudges. But Sorin had not yet had the chance to show his strength and capabilities as a leader. The people approved of him as their crowned prince, but he had yet to be truly tested as a ruler worthy of being king.

"Ahem." Sorin's thoughts were again interrupted, this time by a tall, gangly looking man in fine robes.

Expensive, imported silk from Sagon, no doubt, Sorin thought, with an internal scoff.

"My sympathies to Your Grace, but perhaps this would be a good time for the council to assemble. We were to discuss a rather sensitive subject with His Majesty." He added quickly, "May The Mother carry his soul." The councilman shifted uncomfortably under Queen Evelyn's glare.

Sorin watched as his mother gestured toward the door, "After you, gentlemen."

Sorin caught her elbow as she passed him, "Mother, can we not have even a moment to grieve?"

"I'm sorry my love." She put a warm hand to his cheek. "But the next moves you make will be vital to our survival. Our enemies will be circling and there are things you need to know." She kissed his forehead and, with a signal to her guard, they bounded from the room, leaving the court behind in their wake.

CHAPTER THREE

Sorin

T*he poorly lit chamber always* made Sorin feel as if the world around him were closing in. He had never been comfortable in the stuffy room, and he desperately wished his mother had joined them rather than retiring to her rooms. The council members took their respective seats and remained silent and solemn. The old man sitting across from him was just as dark and drab as the council's chamber. Anselem had always seemed old to Sorin, ever since he first saw him in one of his father's secret meetings at the warehouse. Even as a child Sorin thought there was something different about his father's most trusted advisor. Not that Anselem was a bad man. Despite his appearance, he had quite the jolly temperament.

Anselem raised a hand to address the men around the table. He had been his father's oldest and closest friend, and appeared grief stricken now. Perhaps Sorin was not the only one eager to grieve in the privacy of his own rooms.

Anselem spoke, "Fellow councilmen, we begin this meeting with heavy hearts. King Allerick is gone, and in his place, his only son steps into the light. To carry on his legacy will be no easy task. But know this, *King* Sorin, we will be by your side every step of the way." He choked on his words and cleared his throat before continuing, "We were with your father before the uprising when the people needed us, and just as we were then, we will be with you now." He took a deep breath as he stood and bowed to Sorin. "My hope is that you will trust us as he did."

Sorin knew this was the part where he should say something regal and inspiring. Instead, all he could muster was a "Thank you." He needed to get out of this room, away from all these worried eyes. How could he do this? How could his father leave him so soon and so unprepared? Sorin fought against the bile rising in his throat when another man spoke.

He knew this massive man with a hard-set jaw as well as he had known his own father. General Tyrell was Asterion's military commander. He was also the father of Sorin's closest friend, Sir Bronimir. Sorin and Bron had spent their adolescent years in the training yard with the other soldiers until they were old enough to take the oath with the rest of the Mortal Knights.

The man standing before him now was as hard and unmoving as he had been during Sorin's training. General Tyrell was a gallant but terrifying man and made Sorin feel like he was the same twelve-year-old boy who had been thrown into the dirt and tossed a sword all those years ago. He felt small and unworthy in the general's presence, something he would need to overcome as King.

General Tyrell's voice bellowed loudly, "Now that we have that out of the way, we need to get to the matter at hand."

Straight to the point as usual, Sorin thought with a bitter laugh.

General Tyrell continued with his grave demeanor, "Trade routes to the east in the Living Sea are experiencing trouble in the waters. What was once a tale told by the old drunk sailors seems to be turning into something more substantial."

The others looked skeptical, but Sorin was careful to keep a neutral face. Best not to react until he had heard the rest. He had spent enough time at the docks to have heard stories of Sirens and the occasional Bake-Kuijra, a vengeful spirit who took the form of a skeletal whale. These creatures had mostly kept to themselves with only the rare run-in with Asterion trader ships.

General Tyrell went on before anyone could voice their reaction, "Eleven. *Eleven* ships have been lost in the last two months. Merchants are refusing to set sail again until I have dispatched arms. Even worse, claims of a murderous mist have come in. Even a leviathan attack for Mother's sake. If these claims hold any sort of truth, and I am inclined to believe that they do, then how are my men to fight against it? Against *magical creatures?*"

The air grew tense as Sorin waited to see who would speak out first. He knew it was coming at the mere mention of magic: the narrow-minded, fear-fueled words that would inevitably follow.

Cerwin spoke first. *Shocker, Fancy Pants has an opinion.* Sorin leaned back in his seat, arms crossed, and stormy blue eyes focused on the young councilman.

"You'll find a way, General."

General Tyrell stood, towering over the man, ever the fierce warrior that Sorin knew from childhood. "The chaos headed toward our shores is something my men have never faced. I have been around long enough to know magic when I hear it. That is a power that my men cannot fight on their own. I will not send good soldiers into battle without something to even the playing field."

"Pah!" the gruff, bearded man beside Sorin huffed. Larken was a wise North Skagan man that his father had met in a gambling house before the rebellion. The mountain man now oversaw the Guilds. He was the connection between the builders, farmers, masons, and the like. "I know where this is going. You seek magic to counter the darkness spreading in Asterion. What you are suggesting is madness. To use magic against an enemy we don't even understand yet?" His face was turning red, "Have you forgotten what the Magi did to this country? Sorcerers torching the homes of humans who could not pay that old idiot Idor's taxes? Magi will not be controlled; it is not in their nature. They will always thirst for more power, it is inevitable."

Sorin could not listen to any more of this. These men had come up in an age when Magi were revered by the old king and valued over mortal men. It was true that Sorcerers used power to their advantage, but how easily the councilmen forgot the Hedge Witches who had offered healing in the smaller villages. Or the Mages who kept enemies from the northern shores, who prevented both magical and non-magical attacks on the borders for ages.

It was time for Sorin to step in. He would need to take his place in this sooner or later. One thing he was certain of was that he would make his time on the throne count, no matter how much time that might be. His father had stood up for the common man, but who would he stand for?

Sorin threw a silencing hand up. "Enough. If there is a chance that we can stop this mess from spreading, from hurting anyone else, then we owe it to all of Asterion to explore that option. This land is rooted in magic. It has been from the time that The Mother created it. There is no denying the strength of that power and how it could be of use to us now."

He knew he needed the council's support on this. His father had put this band of men together to keep Asterion's ruling class in check. Sorin had no plans of upsetting that balance, but he also would not stand by while they let their fears control their better judgment.

"My son speaks true gentlemen." Queen Evelyn was standing in the doorway, flanked by her personal guard. She had a hint of pride in her smile as she regarded Sorin. She was dressed in a black velvet gown now with a veil pulled back and away from her face. She must have slipped away to change into her mourning attire while the council settled in, her own show of respect amid all her responsibilities.

She entered the chamber, pushing past a baffled Cerwin. Though Sorin's mother had always played a role in ruling at her husband's side, it was not common for her to be at these meetings. She ignored the indignant stares and spread a large map on the table. It was a map of Asterion, a new version that had just been drafted. Sorin noticed smears of ink; signs that it had been drafted recently, then rolled in a hurry. What stood out immediately was that what had once been open sea to the east was now an area shaded in gray, covering almost the entire trade route to Sagon, their biggest ally and trade partner. Sorin thought it must be the area where ships were being attacked.

Sorin, however, was surprised to see that northern Asterion was shaded as well in the Raven Wood, covering part of Brenmar Lake and stopping just at the Winter Palace.

"What is the meaning of this?" Cerwin asked, though Sorin knew they all had a good guess at the answer.

He could feel the dread creeping in as he voiced his thoughts out loud. "It's not just fisherman tales or random attacks, is it?" It was a blight. On sea and on land. Something sinister was setting in toward the Asterion harbour. Worse, it seemed to be spreading down toward the villages between Brenmar and Aramoor, where Sorin and his father's court resided in the Summer Palace. His heart sank at the thought of all those families. Those villages were the heart and backbone of Asterion, providing the country with crops and livestock.

His mother cut in, "There have been whispers amongst the help regarding animal attacks in the north near Brenmar. Creatures are straying from the forest and, worse, a dense, dark fog has appeared over the lake, black as night. It is the same description as what is being spotted on the trade strait. Fresh water is turning sour in the wells, and crops are withering in the fields."

Sorin was horrified, "Why are we just now hearing of this?"

"When the reports first started coming in, your father suspected dark magic, but wanted to be sure before sharing his fears with the people. He worried that word of this would cause discord in the towns toward any remaining Magi. The moment word gets out, fear will spread, and old wounds will be reopened."

Sorin understood his father's reasoning, but it had left them with little time or preparation for what they were now facing. "If it *is* dark magic, then the general is right, and our army doesn't stand a chance. If this is the work of Dark Magi who are powerful enough to cause a blight, then that means either the relic is not working anymore, or they are more powerful than it is." So many scenarios were running through his mind, he needed time to think.

He thought back to the *History of Magic* books his father had him pore through. Dark magic was dangerous, volatile, and required a great deal of sacrifice. It was powerful but it was also unnatural. Any form of magic required a great deal of balance and respect. Asterion had been formed from natural magic that drew power from nature and the divine. If the land was suffering now, then it needed to be defended. If the books were right, then they would need a Magi connected to Asterion, one who could wield its power in its defense.

His mother said what he was thinking. "We need a Magi to help. We need a *Druid*, someone from one of the ancient bloodlines that are believed to be the first of the Magi kind. If your father's research is correct, then we need a champion born from the breast of Asterion. They would be our only hope."

Sorin pinched the bridge of his nose as his headache returned. To track down one person in an entire continent from a *lost* bloodline... It was insane. And once they did, there would be the matter of convincing that person to abandon everything for a seemingly impossible quest. From the looks on the councilmens' faces, they shared his doubts.

Sorin groaned. *So, this is what it's like to be King.*

CHAPTER FOUR

Shaye

S *haye stumbled into a puddle* of mud; her gray dapple gelding, Finn, pranced at her side trying to avoid any more splashing. His legs were coated in brown just like her breeches and boots. *Perfect*, she thought to herself. *Four weeks on a smelly ship only to find that dry land isn't as dry as I had hoped.* This was the embarrassing state in which she would be seeing her family for the first time in six months. *Makeshift family.* The words crept into her head, uninvited.

It was not fair to think that way. The Erland family had treated her as one of their own from the moment she arrived scared and bloodied, stumbling into their inn at ten years old. That had been merely two weeks after the uprising, but they had not balked at the sight of a Magi child in need. They had fed, clothed, and loved her. They had selflessly raised her alongside their own daughter, Brina, until Shaye was old enough to join the Merchant's Guild.

They had supported her decision to join the Guild and had sent her on her way with a beautiful, embroidered coat, and a pack full of her favorite homemade sweet rolls. She had been so eager to prove herself... To show the world that she was not just another Magi orphan plagued by the trauma of her past.

It had been three years since she had left her home with them at the inn to sail with the Guild, and many months since she had last visited. So much had changed in that short amount of time. She had since then left the Guild to join a less savory crowd from the Padsu Harbour. She supposed in a lot of ways she had changed, too, becoming more comfortable in her own skin. Now, here she was showing up on their doorstep once again, covered in filth. She hoped they would not be disappointed when they heard the news.

"Nervous, love?" Haskell, an exceptionally tall man with light braided hair and a beard to match, put an arm around her as they strolled away from the docks. Finn snorted at him until he drew an apple from his pack. The enormity of her Skagan friend was drawing stares as they walked along the harbour. They strode confidently by the fishermen, ignoring the whispers that their presence invoked.

"Not at all," Shaye lied, ducking from under his arm and raising a brow. "You'd better be careful, Haskell; Asterion doesn't look as kindly on smugglers as Sagon does."

"I'll manage." He scratched his uncombed, bearded face and smiled broadly. "Gonna miss me?"

Shaye took him in for a moment; Haskell was handsome in a brutish sort of way. Although he had tried often, she had never gone to bed with him; but they had been together on the job for so long that she had grown to love him. She loved their entire crew; they were like family. Like a slightly violent, bawdy, criminal family, but family, nonetheless. They had looked out for each other, and it had been difficult to part with them.

"Thank you for coming with me." She smiled warmly at her companion, ignoring Finn's attempts at digging an apple out of the pack she carried. Haskell had volunteered to sail down the coast with her while the others stayed behind in Norbrach. Bidding the crew farewell, she and Haskell had promised to return soon.

"It was nothing. Now go on, I've got a brothel to find." He laughed as he strutted away.

Shaye straightened, swatting Finn's greedy nose away from her pack. "Come on, Finn, time to do what we came here for." They continued down the cobblestone roads, past neat rows of townhouses and shops. She had missed the brightly colored buildings that made up Asterion's capital. Each structure stood warm and welcoming in various hues of yellow, red, and blue. She knew they would be nearing the street to the inn soon, but she spotted a gambling house first. Finn tugged at the reins as she pulled him to a post out front.

"Come on, Finn, just one drink. To calm my nerves." She patted his muscular neck before tying him to the post and feeding him a ripe, red apple. He nodded in approval at the bribe, accepting it.

Shaye turned toward the small wooden building, tucked between two prominent townhomes. It looked out of place here, but no one had ever shut it down. The *Wolves Den* was a seedy, disreputable tavern and her favorite place to go for a game of chance. Inside there were a few men at the bar while others sat at tables playing cards or dice.

The bar was falling apart, the wood chipped and rotting. Shaye wondered why the owner had not invested the money to replace it after all these years. She supposed she had grown too used to the extravagant gambling houses in Padsu, where wealth from all over the world poured into its ports and went to good use to make the town a destination spot for travelers, tradesmen, and even pirates. Padsu, the small harbour in Sagon, had been an exciting and exotic place in comparison to the simple beauty of the Aramoor trade harbour that she called home.

Shaye ordered an ale from the bar, ignoring the bartender who gave her a sly smile before going to help another customer. She rolled her eyes and brushed off her filthy jerkin and breeches, thinking she really should clean up a bit before going home to the inn. She pulled her cascading auburn hair up into a leather string before taking her ale to one of the nearby tables.

She made herself comfortable, and in less than an hour Shaye had collected a nice stack of coins as well as a jeweled brooch, most likely stolen from its previous owner. The Asterion harbor was not known for crime and, for the most part, its inhabitants lived happily. King Allerick had done a fine job of cleaning up the city, and trade had continued to do exceptionally well once he had taken power. He had even strengthened it with the organization of the Guilds. But that did not stop the odd theft from taking place. It was no concern to Shaye, who was racking up her winnings with the loaded dice she had slipped onto the table.

Shaye was laughing at a story the old Skagan man beside her was telling. Skag was a rough country filled with warriors who lived amongst the dangerous mountain terrain. It was someplace she had no desire to visit, especially after his story having something to do with a brothel and a goat. She took a long drink of the sour ale when a commotion at the bar caught her attention.

An old man in a torn cloak was arguing with the barkeep. The burly man behind the bar threw the cloaked man's money back at him. "We don't serve your kind here, Mage. Leave before I show you the door myself." He spat on the floor by the Mage's feet. It was common to see less powerful Magi wandering the city. Many Sorcerers had escaped after King

Allerick took the throne, but Mages and Witches still lingered throughout the city and in the countryside.

Shaye looked at the barkeep in disgust. To refuse service was one thing, but to spit on the floor of your own establishment seemed unnecessary and crude. She had forgotten how ugly the prejudices toward Magi were here in Asterion. Sagon was different in that matter; their king doted on Magi, and you could often find Sorcerers, Mages, and Witches offering their services in various establishments.

The Mage seethed with anger. His hands opening and closing at his side as if he itched to use the magic he no longer had. "I have done nothing to you! I was a border guard for twenty years, protecting ungrateful bastards like yourself from foreign scum."

Sensing things were going to get even uglier from here, Shaye pushed her winnings and loaded dice into her pack and jumped from her seat at the insult. She put herself between the Mage and the offended barkeep before things could escalate further. "Please, Sir, he didn't mean anything by that. We're all on edge, let us share a drink and forget the whole thing."

She placed a few coins on the counter hoping it would be enough to diffuse the situation, but the barkeep shoved them back at her. "Stay out of this."

The Mage scoffed at her, "I don't need your help sweetheart." He shoved Shaye into a nearby stool. This was her thanks for trying to help him.

Shaye clenched her jaw, "I'm not your sweetheart." She picked her coins up from the bar and readied herself to leave.

From the corner of her eye, she spotted a hefty bald man pulling a knife from his belt. Shaye waited for the man to make his move. *So much for calming my nerves. This is what I get for involving myself in this crap.*

The man lunged with his knife at the unsuspecting Mage,

who was still busy spouting insults at the bartender. Ignoring Shaye, the bald man did not see her coming when she swept in from behind, using all her strength to slam his face into the bar. The man went down with a loud crash, taking several bar stools with him. When he stood, his face was a bloody mess where she had just broken his nose. Shaye stepped back, satisfied with herself, before all hell broke loose.

CHAPTER FIVE

Shaye

S *haye left the gambling house* with a bag full of coins, an ornamented brooch on her cotton shirt, and a black eye. Finn walked loyally at her side and nudged her in the arm. "I know, I know. I should have just minded my own business. But you didn't see them, Finn. They needed a little lesson in manners."

Black eye aside, she was feeling rather good about herself and how well she had held her own in the brawl. Haskell would be proud. After she broke the big guys' nose, the rest of the tavern broke out in a fight. She had done a splendid job, although taking a hit to the face had not been her finest moment. Her eye throbbed; she would be lucky if she could see out of it tomorrow.

She looked down and flinched at the state of her clothes; they were bloody and torn. She nudged Finn in the shoulder and laughed, "At least they won't notice the mud now." He whinnied cheerfully in response.

If she had been worried about the state she was going to be in when she arrived at the inn before, now she was really embarrassed. But between the ale and the adrenaline, she had been able to take her mind off the conversation she would need to have with the Erlands when she arrived at the inn. Shaye and Finn followed the cobblestone road into her neighborhood. She waved at a few of the residents sitting on their townhome stoops. They recognized her, calling out and welcoming her home.

She felt giddy at the sight of the inn on the end of the street. As she neared the tall stone building, the familiar scent of the evening's meal filled her nose. It was a delightful smell of roast, slow cooked in fresh herbs and spices. *Home*, she thought to herself. The familiar sights and sounds of the street were the same as the last time she had been there. She could see that business was booming at the inn, with patrons bustling in and out. Smiling couples walked up to the large porch, arm in arm, on their way to dinner in the large, welcoming dining room.

Shaye had adored the inn since the first time she had seen it. Brina's grandfather had built it years ago. He had saved every penny he had ever earned on the docks so that he could build a legacy for his family. When he passed away, he had left it to Brina's father, Rolland. Honored by his father's hard work and sacrifice, Rolland took great care to make the business a success. When the Guilds were created, he was first in line at the courthouse to join.

The Guilds had a special place for business owners and Rolland was one of their greatest advocates. His family had prayed hard for the day when they could make a real difference for the people of Asterion. Rolland had worked closely with the king's council to set up a line of communication between the palace and the people of Aramoor.

Brina's mother, Rebecca, had also done her share of community service. She had planted her own garden after insisting that the tavern could benefit from a little home-grown fare. She was also happy to share their bountiful harvest with neighbors down on their luck, or to sell at a deep discount during the weekend market.

To Shaye's surprise, the garden had thrived in the city. She had loved sitting on the inn's veranda with Rebecca on sunny days. They would spend hours together, tending to the vegetables and herbs, surrounded by the cheerful noise of the town around them.

The city was always bustling with its residents and the traders coming in and out of the port. Used to the quiet beauty of the Winter Palace and unoccupied land surrounding its grounds, Shaye had found Aramoor chaotic when she first arrived as a child. But now, the sounds of sailors leaving and returning to port, merchants haggling, even the drunks shouting nonsense on their way home from the tavern, were all familiar to her.

Lost in the nostalgia of her years in Aramoor, Shaye did not see the big, gray dog coming from around the kitchen entrance. The hound's heavy frame loped up to Shaye, splattering even more mud on her already covered pants. The dog was busy giving Shaye wet, sloppy kisses when Brina appeared. Buckets of dog food hung from her arms, but as soon as she spotted Shaye, she dropped the buckets and came running.

The girls embraced, nearly falling over and spooking Shaye's moody dapple gelding. "You're here! I can't believe it, look at you." Brina stepped back, taking in Shaye's appearance. Shaye felt self-conscious with her disheveled locks and muddied breeches. But Brina beamed at her, "You certainly look the part, don't you? Our world traveler, home with stories to tell, I hope." Brina smiled broadly, tucking a runaway strand of hair back into the neat bun on her honey-blonde head.

She was wearing a simple blue dress with a beautifully

embroidered apron. Rebecca's handiwork, no doubt. Brina had inherited none of her mother's creative skills and much preferred to be in the excitement of the inn or caring for the dogs that they bred on the side for additional income.

Shaye was so proud of the woman Brina had become. They had been close since the moment Shaye had appeared on their doorstep in search of food and a warm place to sleep. Brina had spent countless nights telling Shaye stories of the exotic east and the vast mountains to the west. And on the nights when Shaye would awake from visions of blood and terror, Brina would crawl into her bed, recounting her favorite tales of adventure until Shaye drifted back to sleep.

A young boy peeked his head out of the kitchen door and called to Brina, "We're out of mint!"

"Run down to the market to grab some. We'll need it for the tea. And do not let that old hag overcharge you!"

The boy nodded before running off to do as Brina had bid. Shaye suppressed a smile; Brina was a merchant at heart and could haggle with the best of them. She handled everything from orders to menus, and often discussed improvements she thought her father could make to the inn. Brina believed in stability and order, certain of her place in the world. That was the security the Erland family gave Shaye: order and a place to belong.

Brina frowned at Shaye's eye, which she could feel had swelled to a considerable size by now. "Well come on. Dad has a whole feast planned." She added with a scowl, "And I'll get you something to help with the swelling."

After setting Finn up in the stables, the girls turned toward the large gray stone building, the *Brass Blossom*. They decided to go around the front to avoid the dinnertime rush in the kitchen, where the hired help was doing their best to keep up with the large crowd there for the evening. Shaye touched her hand to the ornamental brass flower that gave the inn its name, hanging beside the wooden door. It felt cool and smooth beneath her fingers.

She could hear laughter coming from inside. It was a full house with travelers from all over Asterion in town for the festivities leading up to the spring festival. It was Aramoor's biggest event of the year; the city would be alive with music for the next few weeks. Shaye smiled at the thought.

Inside, the air was warm and inviting, a nice change from the brisk nights Shaye had grown used to while at sea. The large dining area smelled of roast and herbs. The trappings of a Rolland feast were laid out on the longest table, where the family would dine together tonight. Surrounding the table, throughout the dining area, were smaller tables topped with arrangements of fresh flowers from the garden.

The inn's patrons sat around the tables in good cheer. Families were trying to get children to settle down and eat their dinners, while others who had traveled to the city alone mingled with other guests at their tables. This was one of Shaye's favorite things about the inn. As a child, she and Brina had passed the time by eavesdropping on stories the travelers would tell one another in the common areas.

Her second favorite thing had been the food. Shaye had dreamed almost daily of the food Rolland Erland made. He was an innkeeper first, but a master chef at heart. There was not a dish in the world that the man could not master.

He was a rough-looking sort, the kind of man who had spent every moment since childhood getting his hands dirty, working to survive. But you could be certain that those calloused hands sprinkled love into every meal he made for his friends and family. Shaye was certain he would even stuff his worst enemy to the brim with home-cooked stews and pies. He enjoyed bringing people together over a hot meal; it was how he showed love.

People came from all over the world to try his famous

dishes, and they were never disappointed. Shaye strolled past the long table, grabbing a roll from one of the baskets and popping half of it into her mouth before heading to the sitting room. It was beautifully decorated, each piece carefully curated by Rebecca herself. Paintings adorned the walls and hand-embroidered pillows sat on the couches arranged throughout the room. A few ladies sat, trading gossip on one of the loveseats.

Shaye spotted Rebecca, sitting by the fire alone, knitting needles in hand. A smile spread across her face when the small woman noticed the two girls by the doorway. "She's here, Rolland! Our girl is home at last." Her face beamed with excitement, followed by a frown at Shaye's black eye. "What in The Mother's name happened to you? Are you alright?"

"I'm fine, I promise. It was just a minor incident... An old Mage got himself into some trouble when they wouldn't serve him at the tavern." She did not mention that she had been there all afternoon gambling and drinking.

Rolland dusted flour off his hands, though it did not do much good since it covered him almost head to toe. "More and more of that happenin' around here. People are on edge, turning Magi away from work, even down at the docks."

Brina cut in, petting the big dog at her side, "Father, let's not start Shaye's welcome home off with town gossip." She slipped the pup a treat from her pocket. "Let's eat, we'll all feel better with full bellies."

Once they were finished embracing, they sat to eat. Brina and Rolland caught her up on the latest news in town as Rebecca filled her glass. The conversation died down toward the end of their meal, and Shaye braced herself for the talk that had to come next. She wiped the sauce from her face. *Maybe I shouldn't have eaten that second helping*, she thought to herself, as she prepared to give the bad news.

Before she spoke, she looked around the dining area. Most

of the inn's guests had gone to bed for the night, leaving them with only a few stragglers at the bar. It was getting late, and last call would be announced soon.

Knowing it was better to just come out with it, Shaye took a deep breath, "I've been taken out of commission." She braced herself for their reaction and took the opportunity to slip a dried apricot into her mouth. She savored the sweetness of it as she waited for someone to speak.

Brina jumped in immediately, "If those pig-headed fools think they can push you out of work, then they have another thing comin' to them. How dare they? The balls those men must have..."

Rolland cleared his throat in reprimand and nodded to Shaye to continue, but not before she noticed the smirk on his face. Brina was fiercely protective of the people she loved and quick to turn brazen when riled up. When they were children, Brina had been the smallest girl in their neighborhood, but it had never stopped her from standing up to anyone who teased Shaye for being Magi.

"It's not that. Everyone is out of commission: Sailors, traders, smugglers..."

"Smugglers?" Rebecca looked aghast. Shaye bit her lip; she had not yet told her family what she had been up to in the last six months. She had written to them often, careful not to mention that she was no longer an apprentice in the merchant's Guild. She did not relish the idea of misleading them, but she wasn't sure they would understand why she had done it.

She struggled even now to tell them. "I left the Guild. I..." How could she say this without disappointing or hurting them? "My nightmares were getting worse. The last time I was home I could barely function. You remember, don't you? I was afraid to sleep, plagued by night terrors."

Each of them nodded and Shaye knew they were recalling

how difficult her last visit had been. Her nightmares had been worse than usual. Most nights she would awake in cold sweats, sure that monsters were lurking in the corners of her room. No matter how hard she tried to fight it, her mind would take her back to the ballroom on the night of the Winter Solstice. Each time was the same; her standing helpless in the middle of the chaos, searching the room for Bastian.

On particularly bad nights she would find him, only to watch as one of King Allerick's men plunged their sword into his back. She knew it wasn't real because that night she had not been able to find her friend in the ballroom. He had begged her to stay with him, but they had been separated. She never knew what fate had met Bastian, but she prayed every night to The Mother that he had made it out as she did.

The nightmares had continued to grow worse the older Shaye got. She found herself trying to drown them out with late nights at the gambling houses and with strong ale. Still, they came, and as hard as Brina had tried, Shaye had been inconsolable. Darkness clouded her thoughts even when she had been awake. Her body had become so exhausted that she had begun hallucinating during the day and sleepwalking at night.

One such night, they had found her down by the water, wading in waist deep. In her dream she had been chasing Bastian, calling out to him, begging him to wait for her. But he had never slowed, leaving her behind. When she awoke, Brina and Rolland had been there with terror-filled eyes.

She tried to push down the memory of that night as she went on, "So when I returned to Sagon, I made a choice to stay. I had hoped that by putting distance between myself and Asterion and the memories of the Winter Solstice, maybe I could escape the nightmares." She reached for Rebecca and Brina, taking their hands in hers, "And it worked for the most part.

The dreams were not nearly as bad. I had friends and I was happy."

Rolland cut in, "Shaye, what have you been doing for work?"

"At first I gambled mostly," she said blushing. They had not exactly approved of that pastime of hers, but she had been good at it, able to put herself up in a nice room and to keep herself fed. "Then I met a local girl who said she knew how to make some easy money. All I had to do was help them sail their ship."

"Smugglers," Rolland guessed, shaking his head.

"Yes, and I'm sorry. I promise to explain everything to you, and I promise I haven't crossed any lines; but I need to talk to you about what's happening out there." She pointed toward the harbour. The room was getting colder as the fire began to die out. She crossed her arms trying to warm herself.

She knew how crazy this was about to sound. She had gone through it over and over in her head all the way home. The topic of her origins was rarely discussed. Not because the Erlands did not want to talk about it, but because Shaye preferred to keep those thoughts to her nightmares, not her daily life. She did not want the shadows to creep into her safe space here at the inn, with this family who had accepted her. Unfortunately, this was something she could no longer sweep under the rug.

The Erlands waited patiently as she continued, "Listen, I'm sure by now you've heard talk on the docks. Something is preventing traders from crossing the strait. Ships have gone missing and the stories that are coming back in their place are... Well, they're disturbing, to say the least."

Rolland nodded, "We know. A trader came through here last week. At first, we thought the man was insane... Or drunk." He chuckled, but there was no laughter in his eyes this time. "He was claiming magic was back. That there were

Sirens coming near the shores and that one ship had even been taken down by a Kraken."

"I'm here to tell you, they're not just stories." Shaye's leg shook under the table. Thinking about the attack was making her anxious.

Her family sat back as she gave her own account of the monsters coming up from the deep. Her ship had taken a commission that'd had them sailing from Sagon to Asterion. Their captain had heard the stories and had decided it would be safest to sail around the trade strait and into Asterion's less popular harbour in Norbrach. It was considerably smaller and drew less attention than the one here in Aramoor.

Halfway through the Living Sea, they came across another ship. It had been destroyed, leaving large pieces of debris floating in its wake. Judging from the supplies left floating in the water, it had been a smaller trade vessel, taking supplies to Northern Asterion. In the distance, they could see a thick, dark fog creeping away, and with it they had heard the calls of men pleading for rescue.

Shaye and a few others had begged the captain to go in the direction of the voices, to search for any survivors, but after watching the fog rise and coil with the tide, like a living creature, the old privateer had declined. He ordered the crew back to their posts. They had no choice but to obey and sail away from the wails coming from the dense unnatural fog.

Shaye still wasn't sure if they had done the right thing, but every instinct in her body told her they likely would have met the same fate if they had not continued to Asterion shores that night.

Once they had docked in Norbrach, she bid her friends farewell, promising to return with them once the seas had calmed. They had no idea when it would be safe again, so they agreed to stay in Norbrach to listen for any more reports from ships coming in. If any ships came in at all.

Haskell had accompanied her to Aramoor so he could also listen for word in the south, to see if the harbour in southern Asterion would be safer to set sail from. She also guessed that he had volunteered for the job so he could visit the brothels. Now she was home, to warn her family and anyone who was thinking of taking their chances in sailing on the Living Sea, that it was unsafe.

When she finished, Rolland sighed, his broad body almost folding in on itself in defeat. Something was wrong and Shaye sensed that they did not want to tell her about it.

He scratched at his chin, "Shaye, the thing is, stories have started coming in from the north too. Complaints of crops withering in rich soil, water turning bad, undrinkable in the wells... And things coming out from the Raven Wood."

Shaye was confused. "What sort of things?" She had not been any further north than Norbrach since she was a young girl. She shivered at the thought of that big empty palace, the one that haunted her dreams.

Rebecca finally spoke, "Magical things. Creatures that have not been seen or heard of in over a decade. Spirits, Wraiths, even Naga. They are testing the borders. As for the crops, the weather has been ideal for farming this year. Our friends in Norbrach say they have not lost a single vegetable in their fields. But the villages closer to the Winter Palace are claiming contamination where there shouldn't be."

Shaye winced at the mention of the Winter Palace, the setting of her nightmares. Where she had once fled from screams and pleas of mercy. Everyone knew the stories of the relic responsible for dampening magic in the Kingdom. Its reach stretched from the Raven Wood all the way down to the southernmost tip of Asterion. For over a decade it had successfully kept magical creatures from venturing south of the Winter Palace. If they were pushing the boundary then something was seriously wrong.

Brina slammed her drink on the table, spilling red wine out of the top and onto the tablecloth Rebecca had laid out.

Her face was every bit as fierce as a Wraith itself. "If something is wrong, then it is up to the King to handle it. Why have they not investigated or sent reinforcements to help?" She looked at Shaye, her gaze softening in sympathy at the mention of the king and magic.

Magic was an uncomfortable subject for all of them. Brina's family was human, but they had not thrown Shaye out when they discovered her Magi heritage. She hadn't been able to use her powers anyway so there had been nothing to discuss. The King was an even sorer subject. He had been responsible for the death of her aunt and uncle and countless others. It had been a bloody coup, not a peaceful one.

Shaye had been sent to the Winter Palace as an orphan, forced to live with her aunt and uncle who had never wanted the responsibility of a five-year-old girl. They had immediately sent her off to the Mages to learn the art of magic, but she had not taken to it easily. Maybe it had been the trauma of losing her parents at such a young age, or that she came from an old bloodline, devoid of the sort of power Mages and Sorcerers were experts at wielding.

Not that it stopped the Mages from pushing her in endless hours of alchemy and enchantment lessons. It was on rare occasion that she performed magic successfully, and when she did, it was a mediocre spell at best. It was never anything warranting pride in the Master Mages' eyes.

Brina sat back and crossed her arms, bringing Shaye back to the present, "The old arrogant arse ought to be taking care of this before it gets further out of hand."

Shaye paused and looked at her family as Brina's statement registered with her. How was it that they had not yet heard the news? The town had been buzzing with it when she arrived. "You haven't heard? The King is dead."

The shock of her statement stopped everyone in their tracks. Stunned, Shaye spoke again, "The men on the docks were talking about it. I thought surely word would have already reached you." What was keeping the palace from making the announcement? The people surely had a right to know.

Rolland stood abruptly, shaking the large table in his wake. He walked silently out the door. The women sat at the table, unsure of what to say next. Nosey patrons looked at the table, surely wondering why Rolland had stormed off so suddenly and at such a late hour.

Rebecca cleared her throat, "We all knew he was sick; it was common knowledge, he had been for some time." She took the embroidered napkin from her lap and sat it gently on the table. She placed her hands in her lap and looked down at them. Rebecca believed deeply in The Mother of creation and Shaye knew that she was saying a prayer for the late King.

Brina had no patience for it. "It doesn't matter, mother. If he is gone then Prince Sorin will take the throne. It is a major shift in power, one that the people need to have officially been made aware of."

Rolland returned, breathless like he had been running. He held a parchment with a piece torn from the top as if he had ripped it from where it had hung. The proclamation in his hand had the royal crest stamped at the bottom: a wooden stave crossed with a sword and shrouded with native Asterion florals.

His eyes were filled with grief and his hand trembled. "Shaye is right. These are placed around town. The funeral procession will be coming this way within a day or two. The crowning ceremony is to take place immediately after."

Shaye felt pity for Rolland. His family had been a strong supporter of King Allerick. Rolland had respected him as much as he had respected his own father. The few guests who were still downstairs crowded around him to get a look at the proclamation in his hand.

Shocked murmurs filled the room, and a nearby woman began to cry for their beloved king. Shaye did not join in the mourning of King Allerick; instead, she sat as silent and unmoving as the brass blossom hanging by the door outside. Brina put a hand on her shoulder, showing her support.

Rolland set the paper on the table, his breath was steadier now as he said, "King Allerick is dead. Long live King Sorin."

The room erupted in response, "Long live King Sorin."

Shaye threw back the rest of her drink and wiped her face with her sleeve; without uttering a word, she went up to bed.

CHAPTER SIX

Sorin

S orin hit the ground with a jarring thud. A massive knight shouted at him from across the training yard. "Come on! You've got more than that. You gonna let that runt best you in front of your men?" Bron was getting way too much enjoyment out of this. Sorin rolled onto his side and saw his friend's dark eyes crinkled at the corners in laughter.

"It was a lucky shot!" Sorin shouted back, dusting himself off and preparing for another round with the knight standing across from him.

They had been at it for hours and Sorin was exhausted. A light spring breeze drifted in the air providing the only form of comfort. The training yard was alive with the sounds of steel clashing and men shouting good-natured insults at one another.

Anik rushed him, too boldly, and Sorin knocked the sword from his hand, tossing him into the dirt of the training grounds. Bron joined them, towering over Sorin and Anik. He was laughing at the look of defeat on Anik's face. Sorin helped his stout friend from the ground. "Are you hurt?"

"Only my pride," Anik joked, as he dusted himself off, wiping the dirt from his dark skin. The men around them joined in on their laughter. They had all stopped their training so they could watch their new king square up against one of their most decorated knights. Though he was small, Anik was a fierce fighter and one of the most respected Mortal Knights in the Kingdom.

Sorin shouted to another one of their friends, "Hey Elijah! Let's eat!" The freckled boy stopped what he was doing in the armory and came running. He was the youngest of their little band and had joined them a few years ago as a squire. The fiery redhead had proven himself quickly and Sorin had been impressed, inviting him into their fold.

Bron and Anik, on the other hand, had been with him since childhood. They had grown up together, and their fathers had fought side by side. They had all three trained under General Tyrell in the first army order. During that time, every one of them had excelled, especially Bron, who had been sent for special training, earning the title of Mortal Knight quickly. He lived for a good fight.

And a fight he'll get, Sorin thought. Tonight, he would ask the impossible of them. *Better get them drunk first.*

They ate in the mess hall attached to the barracks. None of them lived there with the other soldiers, but they liked to spend time there, away from the trappings and etiquette of the court.

The men were laughing at Sorin and the idea of him being crowned King. The other soldiers around them would chime in from time to time; but, by now, everyone was deep in their drink. Talk of the blight swarmed the hall. Some men dismissed it as rumor, others were making claims as to which magical creature they would beat in a fight. Sorin did his best to ignore the talk. It was time to make his proposition.

"Remember the time we were stranded in Skag,

surrounded by those idiot mountain men?" His friends smiled at the memory.

"I thought we'd die in that Mother-forsaken country." Bron scratched at his closely shaved head and threw back the rest of his drink.

"But we made it out. Together." Sorin leaned in quietly, growing more serious. "Asterion is in trouble, and I'm in over my head. The only way I'm going to set things right is with the three of you there with me. I know it's a fool's mission and we're going in blind, so I want your honest answers as my friends, *not* as my knights."

"We'd follow you to The Beyond if you asked us to, brother." Anik saluted with his glass and the others followed suit. It warmed Sorin's heart that they were so willing to ride with him. It was hard for him to believe he deserved their loyalty, but he gladly accepted it.

"Then put your affairs in order." He finished his drink, noticing a scantily clad woman in a red dress trying to get Bron's attention. "We leave as soon as the council approves." He elbowed Bron and nodded toward the woman; Bron smirked and held up a finger, signaling her to wait a moment for him.

The men finished their drinks and went their separate ways. Bron and the others had found companions to warm their beds for the night. They had no idea how quickly they would need to leave or how long they would be gone after all. Best to make the most of their time left here.

Sorin went back to the palace, intent on going straight to bed. He could not shake the feeling that he had already failed before he had begun. Doubt had been rearing its ugly head more and more these days. "Damn him," he mumbled under his breath, rounding the corner in the east wing of the Summer Palace.

"Who is it that you're damning exactly, Your Highness?"

Duchess Adella was leaning against his door. She twirled her pale blonde hair and batted her light lashes at him.

"Nobody." He shook his head. "Don't forget, it'll soon be 'Your Majesty.'" He rolled his eyes at the thought. The alcohol was finally catching up to him. He regretted that last drink as he fumbled trying to find the key to his chambers. The hall was empty, the rest of the court had gone to bed hours ago.

"It's your father, isn't it? He's the one who you're angry at." Adella had grown up in the comfort of palace life. Her father had been a duke in the old king's court but had quickly flipped sides when he realized that Allerick had the upper hand. Sorin had always been disgusted by the courtiers who had betrayed their king only to keep their position. Now they lingered in his father's court, eager to win favor and praise from their new king.

"It's this whole damned mess, Adella." He moved to unlock his door, but she blocked his way. She made a pout with her thin, pinched face. He had never thought much of her and the way she held her own court with the ladies around the palace. She acted as if she were entitled to special treatment due to her father's title.

She batted her lashes at him. "You need to let it go. The court talks. We've all heard the whispers that the two of you fought before he passed." She sidled up to him, pressing her thin body against his. "You wanted him to reinstate magic. You're out of your mind if you think the court will allow that to happen."

Anger surged through him. Through gritted teeth he warned her, "Things are different now. Do not mistake me for a fool, Adella. I will not make the same mistakes as the kings before me, and I most certainly will not be swayed away from what is right."

He found his key, unlocking the door to his chambers. He pushed past her, quickly shutting the door behind him and locking it. The room suddenly felt foreign to him. He looked around, grumbling at the pile of papers sitting on the large wooden desk. A reminder of his old princely duties that he had been putting off when his father was still alive.

Sorin felt like a fraud, here in this room and inside of the Summer Palace. He thought about how deeply he cared for the people of Asterion and how they deserved better than him. He was not ready for this responsibility.

"You're going to have to stop thinking like that if you're to succeed, you know." A man's voice came from the balcony. Sorin was not entirely surprised; he did not know if anything would surprise him anymore. Now he really wished he had not drunk so much. He poured himself a glass of water and carried it to the balcony.

"Anselem, it's a little late for a council meeting, isn't it?" Sorin joined him out on the terrace. Little lights could be seen flickering in the city but mostly it was dark. He hoped his people were sleeping peacefully.

Things were going to get worse before they got better, and he prayed they would be able to enjoy themselves a little while longer before that happened. He looked at the old man beside him, who was thoughtfully watching the city as well. "What made you think I wasn't going to return with a woman tonight?" Sorin joked, taking a drink of his water, relishing in the coolness of it.

"Pah, you've got your father's way with women. I knew the chances would be slim." Both men laughed.

"Wanna tell me how you knew what I was thinking in there?" Sorin took another drink of water. The laughter died down then as Sorin allowed Anselem to contemplate how to respond. Sorin took it upon himself to say what the old man was trying to find the words for. His voice was a mere whisper on the night wind, "You're Magi."

Anselem nodded and started to cough. Sorin led him back

into his chambers and poured him a glass of water. "We're going to need something stronger than that, boy." Sorin obeyed and poured them both a glass of mulled wine. *Why stop now?* Sorin told himself. This was going to be an uncomfortable conversation.

"Did my father know?"

"Yes, he did. Young man, I think it is important for you to know that your father never hated us magic users. He only wanted to stop the abuse of our power. We had no idea that the relic would be so effective in stopping the use of magic. The intention had only been to stop the more advanced wielders in the Winter Palace from getting in our way."

"Yet twelve years later, those men are dead, and the Magi are left to be treated like pariahs."

"I know you harbor feelings of hate for what we did that night. I can feel the anger inside of you, toward your father, but also toward yourself. You need to believe you can do better, Sorin. That you *will* do better."

Sorin nodded and rubbed his eyes. He was tired. Tired of the responsibility and the expectations. "I don't suppose you can just tell me exactly what I need to do to set this right?"

"If only it were that easy, my boy. I can, however, tell you that your mother was correct in her research: the Druid will be your biggest hope. Druids were once the most powerful Magi in the land. Their magic is of the purest form, connected to nature and all living things. But as Sorcerers emerged, learning how to manipulate magic, how to grow it beyond its natural capabilities... it left the Druids powerless against any Magi who allowed greed to overtake them. And believe me, the hunger for power and wealth is not an easy thing to resist." Sorin understood what his father's friend was telling him, but he was not sure why it was so important.

Anselem continued, "When you do the research you will find that there is only one Druid left in the official records. I have felt her presence like the first hint of a spring breeze. The girl will no doubt appear powerless. It has been a long time since my kind have felt any hint of magic in these parts. I am only now beginning to feel the faint whisper of the power I used to possess. She is no doubt untrained and will need your help as much as you will need hers. Trust each other and you both just might make it back here in one piece."

Anselem finished his drink and went to the door. It looked as if he would say something else but instead gave a curt nod to Sorin, opening the door to take his leave.

Sorin watched the limp in his gait, and it occurred to him that he had always thought there was a strangeness to the councilman. How he had seemed older than he looked, weary even. He asked him before he could go, "How old are you, Anselem?" An unimportant question, but one that he wanted to ask anyway out of boyhood curiosity.

The old man chuckled, "Too old my boy, too old."

CHAPTER SEVEN

Sorin

They had been working at a breakneck pace between research and preparations, and Sorin was exhausted. The morning after his talk with Anselem he had woken Bron and the others with a decanter of coffee in hand. They had made the most of the night before and had paid for it dearly that morning. They groaned in response to Sorin's request that they help him with his research in the library. It was a task that none of them relished.

Research wasn't the only thing on Sorin's long list of preparations. It had taken days to convince the council to allow his mother to rule in his stead. He had pleaded with them to agree to him taking his small party to find the girl and collect the relic, explaining that sending an army north would draw too much attention. If what they believed about dark magic users was true, then Sorin would need a scouting party he could trust.

Sorin, Bron, Elijah, and Anik were now riding down the main road, surrounded by travelers headed to Aramoor for the festival. Sorin was tired and it did not help that he smelled like a horse's arse. Bron was leading the way into town on his massive warhorse, Altivo. The midnight black, muscled horse was drawing too much attention for Sorin's comfort, but he tried not to worry about that.

Bron tossed a flask at the newly appointed King. Sorin was possibly the first king in Asterion history to be on a quest instead of sending his most trusted knights in his stead. But Sorin had not been born heir to the throne. Nobody had ever groomed him to do things a certain way and he certainly was not about to start now. Once his father had taken the throne and crowned him as the Prince of Asterion, Sorin had found that he preferred training in the yard with the other soldiers to sitting in a stuffy room replying to foreign correspondents.

Even the crowning ceremony had been very unking-like, consisting of a few words and blessings from a jewel-adorned priestess in front of the court. There had been no grand ball in celebration afterwards, as was the custom in Asterion's past. Instead, his mother had organized a large feast for the court and the foreign emissaries who resided permanently at the Summer Palace, excusing her son from attending, as he'd had to meet with stranded sailors from both Skag and Sagon.

It was all a cover of course, so nobody would suspect what he was really doing. His mother had sent Larken and Cerwin in his stead to meet with the tradesmen, dressing one of their attendants in Sorin's kingly garments in hopes that anyone watching would believe that he had gone with them.

He had full faith in his mother as regent, believing without a doubt that she could handle ruling for a while longer. She had done an impeccable job of it over the years by his father's side, advising him in all major decisions. She knew the formalities and enjoyed being helpful. Most of all she understood that right now nothing was more important than getting their trade routes opened back up and the blight off their land. Even if it meant allowing her only beloved son to run headfirst into the danger.

So, with everything set in place, they now found themselves on their way to get a girl. Not just any girl, but one with an ancient link to the land itself. Sorin wiped his brow with the back of his hand. This was ridiculous. He felt like a fairytale knight off on an impossible odyssey. Real life was messy, there was no magical fix. At least not in the Asterion he had been raised in.

His mother had made a good case for taking this course of action. Even the council had unanimously agreed that this was their best chance. Just as Anselem had predicted, the records had stated that she was the last of her kind, as far as they could tell. Weeks of searching the dusty archives had shown that there had been a young girl, who had come from just such a line, in the palace before the uprising.

His father was a meticulous record keeper and they discovered that she had fled the uprising, ending up down south in the Aramoor harbour district. How someone so young had managed that he could not imagine. She had been registered by a successful family there as one of the orphaned Magi.

His father had insisted on the registration. He had claimed it was his responsibility to make sure that the children were relocated and safely cared for, integrated into the new non-magical society he had created, and had hoped it would be enough for a smooth transition.

Sorin recalled the meetings he had attended as a young boy. They had been held in safe houses down by the docks. The plan had been simple at first; surprise the old king's court on their most beloved celebration of the year. His father would take a group of supporters there to make their voices heard and to damage the regime beyond repair by taking the King prisoner. All so that he could take the crown and craft a whole new Asterion. An Asterion that stood for the people, *all* its people. Sorin had heard countless speeches and endless accounts of the atrocities the old king and his Magi had committed on anyone who had spoken out against their abuses of power. All Sorin could hope for now was that the girl was alive and well, and not the type to harbor a grudge. He rolled his eyes and cursed out loud.

"Where's your head?" Bron cut into Sorin's thoughts.

Sorin took a long swig from the flask. Whatever was in it burned deeply. "Oh, you know, just wondering how I ended up here on this smelly brood, riding alongside a stubborn ass."

"Whoa, don't talk about my horse that way."

"I wasn't talking about the horse," he laughed, throwing the flask back to his friend.

Bron took a drink and gestured around them, "You mean you're not enjoying our little adventure into town? Perhaps you should have left this job to the *real* knights. Just think, you could be sitting around your cozy palace, making plans with those stubborn old owls as we speak."

"Ah but you forget, *I* am a man of the people." Sorin puffed up his chest, doing his best impersonation of General Tyrell. "A good King goes headfirst into battle with his men."

"Except this isn't a battle. This is a kidnapping mission."

Sorin rolled his eyes. "This girl may very well hold the future of Asterion in her magical hands. And we most certainly will not be kidnapping anyone. She must come with us willingly."

Bron scoffed, "There are so many things wrong with this plan. One day they'll write a tragic comedy about it to perform in theatres around the world. Just think: *The Tale of King Sorin and His Knightly Ass.*" Anik and Elijah chimed in with laughter and Bron continued, "Sorin, who's to say the girl is even going to be there. It has been years; she could have moved on, she could be dead for all we know. And say she *is* there, why in The Mother's name would she help us? We expelled her people and slaughtered her kin. Wounds like that run deep. Those sorts of scars don't fade."

He was right. Sorin had been running over every possible scenario in his head since the moment they left the Summer Palace. "You think I don't know that?" He ran his hand through his hair, wishing he would have cut it before they left. "What other option do we have? It has been weeks since my father's death, and I have not even had a moment to grieve, yet here I am off on some ridiculous mission with the lot of you. It's not like I have another relic I can whip out to save the day. The fact that my father found that damned thing in the first place was a miracle. And those old *owls* you speak so fondly of, have no alternative ideas of what to do either."

He paused long enough to notice the city coming into view. They would be approaching the merchant's district soon. The day had been warm and the roads had been crowded. He was ready to get into a soft bed. "I'll be honest with you boys. I don't have a whole lot of faith in this little adventure of ours. If anything, it's a chance to get away from the hopeful eyes at court. I need to *think*. I need to get my bearings on this whole thing. I mean really, *King*? King of a dying Kingdom. I didn't even have a chance to mess it up myself."

They made it into town by nightfall. The stars gazed down at them lighting their way. Asterion was the land of stars, famous for its open skies, its Northern lights, and its magic. At least, it had been.

They checked into a rickety old tavern where the innkeeper eyed them warily. Sorin had decided it would be best if they donned modest clothing, hoping it would help them go unnoticed, as they were doing their best to appear as farmhands headed to the docks for a few nights of ale and girls. Sorin had to admit that Bron looked ridiculous in farmer's trousers and boots instead of his usual armor, and

Elijah kept readjusting the straw hat he had insisted on buying from a peddler on the road.

The men sat at a cramped table full of crumbs from the last guests who had eaten there. They kept their packs with them, worried that the locks on the doors to their rooms would not hold against thieves wandering through town. Girls paraded through the dining room, complimenting lonely men in hopes that they could make some extra money off them.

Bron leaned back in the rickety seat he had taken. "A King's fortune, and this is the best you could do?"

Sorin laughed, "Beats sleeping outside." They had stayed in plenty of places like this before during their time with the military. They had often traveled on patrol, settling any unrest, and checking in on any rumor of black magic use.

Elijah hiccupped, already drunk from the strong ale. "Does it?"

The men laughed and shoveled down the drab food that was being served, having their fill of porridge, no doubt left over from that morning. It was dry and required a great deal of mead to swallow. Sorin forced it down, giving the innkeeper's wife a grateful smile as she slopped a second helping onto his plate. He nodded his thanks, thinking it was best not to offend her, especially when they weren't sure of how long they would be staying. He ate half of it before setting it aside. Anik was across from him struggling with a stale piece of bread. The tavern was packed with people traveling from all over the continent for the famous springtime festival.

The patrons drank and danced well into the night. When Sorin excused himself to go to bed, his men were still drinking and singing with the other guests. Elijah had been roped into a dance with a haughty woman, old enough to be his mother. She was wearing his straw hat and leaving smears of red lipstick on him as she kissed his cheeks. Sorin shook his head and chuckled to himself as he made his way to his room.

The sounds of fighting and laughter drifted up through the thin walls for the better part of the night. Sorin laid in the rock-hard bed, gazing at the stars through the crooked broken window. He wasn't sure how long it was before he drifted off to sleep, but that night, he dreamt of something he had not thought of in a long time. He dreamt of a girl with golden eyes. A girl he had not thought of in many years, with long chestnut hair tied in a ribbon, her face rosy, with tear-stained cheeks. The girl he had risked everything to save.

CHAPTER EIGHT

Shaye

S haye awoke with a start. She was drenched in sweat, and tears were streaming down her face. She had forgotten where she was, for just a moment. Looking around the familiar room, she grounded herself and calmed her breathing. In her dreams she had been somewhere else far away, in that golden snow-fallen palace, where music played, and people laughed. It had been a place that had felt both foreign and familiar to her. It was a dream that visited her often, ever since she was a young girl. In it she had been following a familiar voice.

Bastian had been calling to her. He sounded so close, but she could not see him. It was always the same in these dreams: he always eluded her. Before her, in the candlelit ballroom, people danced, a swirling blur of lace and glitter. They wore beautiful jewels around their necks and on their wrists.

Somewhere beyond the dance floor and the laughter she could hear Bastian's voice calling to her. People twirled around her; delight filled their voices. But when she looked into their faces, tears of blood streamed from their frightened eyes. One woman looked as if she were screaming, though no sound left her lips. Fear flooded through Shaye as she stood frozen in place.

A hand grabbed her wrist, startling her into motion. It pulled her from the ballroom floor and into a stairwell past bloodied guards. Their throats were slit as they laid slumped on the marble floors. She shut her eyes tight as she allowed herself to be pulled past them. Bastian must have finally found her; she would be safe now. But when the boy turned to look at her, she realized it wasn't Bastian. Terror clouded his dark, stormy blue eyes. He was not much older than her, though he was much taller. He held a finger to his lips and then she awoke.

"Another nightmare? I thought they had gotten better. Was it the same as before?" Brina was standing over her, coffee in hand, concern written all over her freckled face.

Shaye smoothed down her hair and looked up at her friend through bleary eyes. "They *were* getting better. I don't know, maybe coming home was a bad idea." She cleared her throat, trying to shrug off the feeling of being back in that ballroom. She did not want to worry Brina over things they could not control, especially on their favorite day of the year. "I'm sorry, I didn't mean that I'm not glad to be home with you. I just... listen, I am fine, I promise. Between all the talk last night of gloom and doom, and your dad's home-brewed mead, I was bound to have a nightmare or two." Shaye rubbed her temples. It had been an exceptionally strong brew last night.

Brina could see through her. "Shaye, I understand you're angry. With the past, and with the late king. It is not fair, what you have had to endure. You have been dealt shit cards, but you need to try to heal. Holding onto that anger and hate is only inviting the darkness in. If you cannot forgive *them*, then you at least need to try to forgive yourself. You did nothing wrong in surviving."

Shaye looked up at the ceiling, noticing the faded stars she and Brina had painted when Shaye had first come to them. She had missed the northern sky and Brina had wanted to give her a little piece of her former home. Shaye looked at her dear friend, the girl who had become like a sister to her over the years. She appreciated where Brina's heart was at, but Brina still could not truly understand. Shaye was Magi and with that came a sense of powerlessness in Asterion.

Magi all over Asterion had to live without a piece of themselves; their magic had been as much a part of them as their soul. Not to mention how easily mortal men would turn on them, just like the Mage in the gambling house who had only come in for a drink and left with a bloodied face instead.

Brina must have picked up on Shaye's shift in mood because she smiled and squeezed Shaye's arm softly. Shaye pointed to Brina's dress, which was covered in dog fur. "Did you sleep in the kennels again?" Shaye frowned at her.

Brina's cheeks turned red. "Only because Missy is about to have a litter of pups. She struggled last time, so I want to be there with her." Brina cared for her dogs like they were her children. She doted on them and spoiled them, much to Rebecca's dismay, as she would rather Brina be married with a litter of babies of her own.

"Oh! Coffee." Brina winked, changing the subject. "Ma has *quite* the day planned for us. We get to help decorate the square. And you get to see Leif. He's finally grown into those ears." The girls laughed and Shaye threw a pillow at her before Brina turned on her heels, and called behind her, "Welcome home, Shaye!"

Welcome home, indeed, Shaye laughed, as she took a long sip of the bitter coffee. She put on a simple dress that she had left behind in the old wardrobe. It had been one of her favorites, comfortable enough, though she would rather wear pants. She glanced at herself in the mirror, trying to smooth down her bedhead. *It'll have to do.* She shrugged and ran out of the room.

Downstairs in the dining area patrons sat groggy at the tables, the result of a late night of celebration no doubt. The spring festival was Aramoor's biggest event of the year. It was a three-day celebration of new life and prosperous crops. But more than that, it was an excuse for music, dancing, and drinking. She smiled at the guests and topped off everyone's coffee before heading to the kitchen.

To her delight, Rolland had made fresh blueberry muffins. The kitchen smelled divine and happy patrons talked quietly nearby. She popped a plump strawberry in her mouth, enjoying the sweet tartness of it. Then she grabbed a muffin and an apple and bounded out the door headed to her first stop to check on her boy.

Finn had been by her side ever since they found each other in Sagon a few years ago. She had won him in a bet while they were docked in the Padsu harbour. He was the only thing she truly cherished in this life aside from Brina and her family. She had taken him as a sign of good luck and a sign that she should follow her gut and leave the Asterion merchant's Guild to stay in the East.

She was nearing the stables when a loud crash came from within, and she heard Finn's panicked whinnies. Before Shaye could reach the door, the largest man she had ever seen stepped out. He was dressed in a rough linen shirt and trousers that were at least one size too small, a sad and obvious attempt at masking who he was. Or *what* he was, Shaye thought, *Soldier*. She backed up a step.

"I don't know what you're doing here, but I'm guessing it's not to attend the spring festivities." Shaye laughed, trying to sound more confident than she felt. If word had somehow gotten out that she had arrived via smuggler's ship, then no doubt they were here for her. It was an offense that would mean jail time, something she was willing to do just about anything to avoid. It was common knowledge that jailors did not take kindly to Magi in their care.

The stranger barked out a laugh, his brown eyes crinkling at the corners. "You don't know me very well, or you'd know I would never pass up a good party." He winked at her, and she considered throwing up a vulgar gesture at him.

Before she had a chance, another man rounded the corner. "What Sir Bronimir is trying to say is that he never passes up the chance to get piss drunk and serenade his closest friends in an embarrassing ballad."

The man, slightly shorter than the captain but still considerable in height, gave a small bow to Shaye. He was handsome in a charming, clean-cut sort of way. He was the type of man she usually steered clear of. The type of man that was entitled and pampered for most of his life. He was more likely a knight than a common foot soldier, she guessed, and most certainly not someone they would deign to send after a small-time smuggler like her. She relaxed slightly, but eyed them warily.

"Well then he'll want to stay away from the mead. It's a lot stronger in these parts than it is up at the palace." She was stalling until she could figure out how many of them there were. They did not seem particularly tense, but she couldn't possibly imagine what two Mortal Knights from the Summer Palace would be doing in the stable of the *Brass Blossom*. Maybe they *were* just here for the festival. She chided herself, *I really need to stop spending time with criminals, it's making me paranoid.*

The second man took a step closer, and Shaye found herself staring at him. He was incredibly handsome, with golden sun-kissed hair grown out of its normal military fashion. His nose was slightly crooked like he had broken it in a fight and had not let it heal right. But he had a strong jaw and carried himself confidently. And his eyes... There was something familiar about them.

She was looking at him so intently that she did not notice the other two men that were now flanking her. She had stalled too long and now she was trapped. She wanted to kick herself for being so careless. Her heart began to pound, and she looked around for something she could use to defend herself should the need arise.

If they knew she was Magi, then they might mean to try their luck in an attack. It was not uncommon for Magi girls to be harassed by the morally tainted men who passed through town. She shifted her gaze between them. Perhaps they had been sent by the palace to question Magi about what was happening in the North and in the Living Sea. She tried to steady her breath; panicking would do nothing to help her out of this.

"I'm sorry milady, we forget our manners. I am Sorin." He swept a dramatic bow this time, taking another step closer. He was close enough now that he could grab her if he wanted to, but he would have to be quick. Shaye had dealt with worse during her time at sea and she was not one to go down without a fight.

"*Ahem. King,* Sorin," Sir Bronimir smiled broadly. Shaye counted the weapons the men had carelessly hidden on them.

"King?" Shaye scoffed. "Sure, and I'm the Princess of Sagon."

Sorin bowed mockingly, "Well Princess, I'm looking for someone. She was registered here as a Magi orphan after the uprising. I assure you, we're only here to talk." He flashed an arrogant smile. Shaye was getting annoyed. For a moment she considered throwing the muffin at him.

"Sure. The knife strapped to the giant's boot *screams* polite conversation, and the two, armed men behind me suggest tea and cookies." Her jaw twitched, she was losing her patience and they were wasting her time. It was midway through the morning and Brina was expecting her in the square.

"Are you offering?" The man claiming to be the King cut through her thoughts.

"Offering what?"

"Tea and cookies." Sorin winked. He *winked* at her. Her face flushed at his arrogance.

What is going on here? What did I just stumble into?

"Please, miss..."

"Shaye, just Shaye."

"Shaye. Please give me just ten minutes; hear me out. We've come all this way." He gestured toward the inn.

"Fine. But *you're* making the tea." Shaye spun on her heel and pushed past the other two men who had been awaiting their orders. They looked at her in shock and confusion as she led them inside the inn.

CHAPTER NINE

Sorin

The inn was spacious with big, handcrafted tables and carefully curated furniture in the sitting room. There was a cozy air to it, reminding him of the comfort he had felt as a young boy. It was a home. Not that the palace was not a beautiful place to live, but it was not the same as the home he had known as a child. The room here was adorned with paintings of exotic lands, with sandy beaches and rolling valleys. It was obvious that great care had been put into choosing them. Flower-filled vases sat in the center of each table in the dining area. It was so unlike the inn that they had stayed in the previous night. Even the patrons were cleaner and more pleasant to be around.

Sorin helped himself to the kitchen, grabbing a tray of teacups and a few tarts that were sitting on the long oak table in the center of the room. Even the kitchen had a home-like quality to it, with lavender hanging from the ceiling to dry and charming ornamental teacups sitting on a shelf. He could see why the Erland family had done so well for themselves with the inn.

Once the tea was brewed, Sorin returned to the dining area where Shaye and his men sat tense and quiet. They had taken up a spot at the longest table, offering a safe distance between her and his armed men. *Clever woman*, he thought. He still had not explained why he was there, and he did not blame her for taking caution.

Bron was staring off to the side, whistling, while Anik and Elijah shifted uncomfortably in their seats under her glare. They were all clearly unsure about what they should talk about in his absence. He handed a small cup to the stubborn girl, "Tea, as promised, milady." He sat down to the side of her, as she had taken the head of the table for herself.

She had not been joking; she really had made him put the tea on. It was bold of her, though he had to admit, he was completely amused by her ferocity. She glared at him with her stunning golden eyes. They were ablaze like the hilt of a sword. It was not uncommon for more powerful Magi to be born with some sort of marking, as a sign of the magic they held within. But it was not the sign of power that caught his attention. It was the memories that flooded him when she looked at him. He would have recognized those eyes anywhere.

When he had come around the stables and had first seen her standing defiantly in front of Bron, he had recognized her immediately. It took every ounce of self-control not to show the shock he was feeling. She had not shown any sign of recognition toward him either, so he was still trying to figure out if she was keeping it to herself as he was.

"So, you're searching for a Magi?" she inquired, taking a long sip of her tea. "There's no shortage of those here, especially with the festival upon us."

The sun was coming in through one of the windows, highlighting the blush on her cheeks. He wasn't sure if she was blushing from annoyance or out of amusement at their presence.

"We are." He set his tea down. It tasted awful, like bitter herbs, and even the cinnamon he had added was not enough to mask how horrible it was. It was the first time he had ever made tea and it showed. "An incredibly special Magi. A *Druid*, if we are being specific. A girl by the name of Shaye Wistari." He raised an eyebrow at her.

Shaye went stiff but kept her face neutral. She was not at all what he had expected. He remembered a small, terrified girl who had trembled, tears streaming silently down her rosy cheeks, while they hid in that dark stairwell. She had clung to him as the sounds of slaughter filled their ears. He took a deep breath to steady himself at the flashback.

"You are the daughter of Caldor and Yrlissa?"

"Wait, what do my parents have to do with anything?"

"Our history books trace bloodlines both human and Magi throughout the ages. Your mother's bloodline, *your* bloodline, is one of the most ancient in all of Asterion history, dating back to some of the first Magi recorded in our books."

Bron spoke up, "What he's trying to say is that things are going to shit. And we need your help."

"Thank you, Bron, helpful as usual." Sorin turned to Shaye. This was going about as well as he had imagined. "He's right. By now you have heard the stories. Our men have seen it themselves out on patrol. Animal attacks are becoming more frequent in the North, attacks that resemble the work of creatures we thought to still be trapped in the Raven Wood. If the relic is losing its power or if something has gone wrong with it, then we need to fix it before more chaos ensues. I know that we have no right to ask for your help after what you and your family have been through—"

"Been through? *Your Majesty*, do you have any idea what it is like to lose your home, not once, but *twice*. To have to run away from the slaughter of your people at just ten years old. Alone and afraid?" Shaye's breath was growing more rapid. Her cheeks were flushed and Sorin sat forward in concern. She looked like an animal cornered in a hunt, and he could tell she wanted to get away from these men who had the nerve to ask *her* for help.

The people around them began to stare as she raised her voice. Sorin needed to calm her down before she made a scene and gave the guests anything to gossip about in town.

She sputtered, "I admit that I harbor no love for the late King Idor, but after what your people have done to mine... Sure, you leveled the playing field for the mortal man, but what of the lower caste Witches and Mages. They were not benefiting from the power and gain of the old regime. They were innocent, and in return they have suffered, stripped of the power given to them by birth. Now they're looked down upon in this *new society* your father created." She took a steadying breath; her hands were shaking, Sorin's concern for her grew.

"You want my help? I have no magic. I never learned the art of alchemy, never had the chance to study the ancient texts. Even when I *was* in training at the palace, I was a pitiful student. You've got the wrong girl." She added with a bitter tone, "*Your Majesty.*"

Sorin suddenly felt ridiculously small. He had been so focused on a solution to a problem he did not fully understand, and had never considered how absurd it would be to ask her for help. She had lost her home and her family because of his father's actions. But he was desperate. There was no hint in any of the palace books at how to fix the relic or how to find something with enough power to replace it. With next to nothing to go on, all he could hope for was that the scorned woman in front of him would somehow be the answer.

"I'm sorry, Shaye. I cannot take back the actions of my father or those of King Idor. All I can do now is to make sure no one else gets hurt. If there is any bearing to these reports regarding the danger that is spreading through Asterion, then I will do whatever I can to stop it." He had to make her understand. "Even if it means coming here, to you, and opening old wounds. I'm sorry, but I don't know what else to do."

He would beg her if he had to. It had occurred to him that this could not be a coincidence. That the girl he saved had grown to be the woman that could save *him* and his country in their time of need. Some would call him naive, but he would not deny his belief in destiny.

A bucket clattered to the ground and the group sitting around the large oak table turned to the entrance of the kitchen. A small, angry woman with wavy blonde hair stood in the doorway, eyes wide and jaw clenched. She took one look at Shaye's trembling hands and grabbed the axe beside the fireplace. "You men have *no* business here. I suggest leaving promptly."

Sorin's men rose in shock at the short woman standing before them, axe in hand. Bron looked as if he did not know whether to laugh or to draw his sword in defense. He looked to Sorin, awaiting an order.

Shaye rose too, stepping between the woman and Sorin and his men. "Brina, uh, meet Sorin. *King* of Asterion." Shaye widened her eyes in a silent plea for her friend to lower the weapon.

Brina paled and dropped the axe. She gave an impressive curtsey that would have rivaled that of any courtier, then turned to her friend. "Shaye, are you okay? I was worried when you didn't meet me in the town square. What are they doing here?" Now whispers were filling the room. A few guests had even risen from their seats to get a better look at the scene unfolding before them.

"I'm fine. These impeccably dressed gentlemen were just dropping in on their way to the spring festival. They'll be leaving now." She gave Sorin a pointed look.

Sorin nodded his head, conceding to her. He was not going to convince her here and now. They had already drawn too much attention. He would have to try again later, preferably when an angry axe-wielding woman was not glaring at him.

He and his men bowed to the spirited women and took their leave. Sorin had known that this would be a challenge, but that did not stop him from shaking his head in disbelief. He made a silent plea as they left the inn: *Fates help me.*

CHAPTER TEN

Shaye

After the men took their leave, Shaye explained everything to Brina. They had excused themselves to their room after reassuring their customers that it had all been a big misunderstanding. Once in the privacy of their room, Shaye began to laugh hysterically, the memory of Brina wielding an axe at the *King* fresh in her mind. It was all so unbelievable, she felt more like she was telling a fisherman's tale in an ale house rather than telling her best friend about her morning at home.

"The nerve of him to come here and ask you to help him." Brina was braiding flowers into Shaye's hair for the festival. She had insisted that they still attend to get their minds off things. She continued, "And was it really necessary to bring the big guy? Were they *trying* to be intimidating?" Brina rolled her eyes.

After a moment she spoke again, "On the other hand..." She paused, and Shaye could tell she was nervous about what she was going to say next. "What are the chances of a king coming here and asking for *your* help? Maybe he is right; I mean, you know that your parents were from the North Pass. Druids were said to have held ancient powers gifted from the land, given by The Mother herself. And he *must* be desperate, seeking you out like this." Brina had always loved stories and telling them to Shaye. It was her childhood tales of Sagon that had prompted Shaye to sail there years later. As soon as Brina had found out where Shaye had come from, she had dug up every story she could find on the ancient Druids.

Surely this was all like living in one of those stories she was so fond of. But Shaye did not share the sentiment. She was nothing like the heroines in those stories. People did not write ballads about girls who cheated at dice and got into barfights.

"It's true, but I don't have access to my magic. Even if I did, I would have no idea how to wield it." She looked down at her hands, which were slightly calloused from her time on the ship. They were the hands of a commoner, not of a powerful Magi with a great destiny awaiting her. "And the relic, by The Mother... Nobody has ever even seen it, aside from King Allerick. King Sorin will be going into this mission blind."

"You're right. But if you were to go with them..." She paused and looked around as if someone might be listening.

Shaye lowered her voice to a mere whisper. "I would know where it is. And could keep them from fixing it." Shaye had dreamed of it before, of magic returning to Asterion, but to say so out loud like this was treason, punishable by death.

"Exactly, it must have crossed your mind. If you destroyed it, then magic would be restored." Brina had never feared magic the same way Rolland and the older generation in Asterion had. She had been so young when it was abolished that she did not know of a time when it had been a danger to humans such as herself.

"I can't even begin to imagine what that would look like anymore. As a child, all I wanted was to feel some sort of power and control. But now, after all this time... For all we know it could start another war." something Shaye would never wish on the country that she still called home.

Brina nodded, finishing with Shaye's hair, she sat down beside her. "On the other hand, with Magi able to wield power again, they would be able to stop this blight, or whatever... Whoever, might be causing it. You wouldn't even need your own power; you would just need to give the power back to *them*."

"But who would keep them from seeking revenge? Stop them from turning against the people who deserved a voice but didn't get one?" She bit her lip at the thought of any more bloodshed and chaos. "I can't deny that the Guilds have been Mother-sent. That they have helped our country prosper, even given *me* purpose at one time. But I would be a liar if I said I hadn't dreamed of revenge more than once." She frowned, looking out the small window in their room and out onto the streets below.

Shaye had once hoped for vengeance against the men who had led the massacre at the Winter Solstice, and she supposed some small part of her that resided in her nightmares still craved it... Until moments like this, with her best friend, a mortal, who had always been there for her. It was like an endless battle raging inside of her, between her two worlds.

"You're right. It would be chaos." Brina flopped down on the quilted bed. "It's like Asterion can't win. No matter what, someone suffers."

Realizing the time, both girls finished getting dressed for the festival. Rebecca had gifted them both with the most beautiful dresses. Shaye ran her hand over the soft floral linen, admiring the small roses and the way the fabric accented her full figure without fitting too snuggly. Brina squealed in delight at the sight of the two of them in the mirror, then led Shaye downstairs where Rolland and Rebecca were waiting for them. They looked festive in their best attire. Even

Rolland was sporting a daisy, pinned to his jacket. Shaye beamed at the happy couple standing before them.

She wondered what they would think of the visit from the King, but she and Brina had decided it was best to save that discussion for after the festival. She wanted just one more carefree day with her family before she had to face any tough decisions.

"You girls look so lovely." Rebecca handed them each a basket of pastries to carry to the square. Every year they set up a tent in the marketplace to sell Rolland's sweets and any fruits or vegetables they could spare.

With word of the blight spreading, Rebecca had decided to offer their goods at a deeply discounted price, claiming that it was their duty to share what they could with their neighbors during times like this. She had always been kind and thoughtful in that way. Though they lived in the largest city in Asterion, the community here was tightly knit. If someone was sick, their neighbors would tend to their business, lending a helping hand however they could. If another had fallen on hard times, the people in town would collect any spare coin they could find.

Shaye had missed that while she had been in the East. Things were more cutthroat there in the Pasdu harbour where she had set down her new roots, with every business in competition with one another. Some even went so far as to sabotage businesses that were doing better than their own. Not that she did not sometimes enjoy watching how creative some of them could get, but she would never admit that out loud.

The four of them wandered down to the festival, arm in arm. Brina was talking nonstop about Leif, the butcher's son, and how handsome he had become in the last few years. Shaye smiled, only half paying attention to her best friend. She was distracted by thoughts of King Sorin. She wanted to dislike him and everything he stood for, but she could not stop blushing at the memory of him bringing her tea. She had not expected him to do as she had bid, and it had surprised her. He was not at all what she had expected, different from the Prince she had heard gossip about. And she had a nagging feeling that there was something familiar about him, she just could not pinpoint what it was.

Growing up, she had heard stories about the royal family. How the young princeling preferred shirking his duties. Instead, spending his days gallivanting with his father's soldiers on patrol or bedding the spoiled ladies of court.

Part of her desperately wanted to believe that, regardless of his past, maybe he would bring a fresh outlook to the throne. If she gave him a chance, then maybe he would look differently upon the Magi he now ruled over... Something she could not do if she denied his request for her to accompany them north.

"We're here!" Rolland announced, as they approached their tent. Familiar faces gathered around in greeting. Some welcomed Shaye home from her long time away, hugging her and asking all about her grand adventures. She talked with them for a while, asking about their families and how their businesses were doing. Many of them had watched her grow up with Brina, and Rolland's position in society had shielded her from a lot of the animosity that other Magi were faced with.

"Let's go see what sort of trouble we can get into!" Brina pulled her away and into the lively crowd, toward the music playing in the beautifully decorated square.

CHAPTER ELEVEN

Sorin

T*he square was covered* in flowers and streamers. The spring festival had always been a popular affair. It was magnificent really, how the whole city had been decorated to create the very image of spring itself. Daffodils and tulips lined the streets and vendors from all over the countryside stood, selling airy fabrics for the upcoming heat and fresh fruit new to the season.

Lively performers danced and sang in the square, their faces flushed from the sun. Sorin had decided to stay in his modest clothing, insisting his band of merry men do the same. He did not want them to draw attention or cause alarm; the mere size of them was enough to draw the odd glance. He strongly felt that the people needed to celebrate, and he did not want to ruin the festival for them.

An elderly woman, wrinkled from many years in the fields, offered him a cool refreshment from her stand. He graciously accepted, paying her generously, and looked around for Shaye. He still was not sure if she had any recollection of him, but he had never forgotten her. Twelve years had passed since that night and though she had grown into a beautiful, full-figured woman, she still had those same piercing, golden eyes hooded in long, thick lashes.

Those eyes visited him in his dreams often. Some nights they smiled at him, other nights he saw the same terror from that cold winter's night. He could still feel the fear that had filled him as he had pulled her into a nearby stairwell, urging her to take a servant's passage out of the palace. He had been so intent on getting her away from there and the horror that awaited everyone in the ballroom.

Although he had been only a few years older than her, he had understood the severity of what that night would bring. His father had been honest with him about the fallout that would come after, and Sorin did not know if it was instinct or something more that had made him lead her to safety beyond the palace walls. It had only been once they reached the lake that he had urged her to run on without him, allowing him enough time to return to the ballroom before his absence was noticed.

Someone tapped him on the shoulder, interrupting the distant memories. He smiled at the bright-eyed women standing in front of him. Both Shaye and Brina had flowers braided into their hair. Shaye's waist-length, russet hair shined bright under the sunlight, intertwined with yellow and red rose buds. She smiled ruefully at him. "Nice clothes, *Your Majesty*. Playing farm-boy for the day again?" She raised her eyebrow at him, and he found himself blushing in response.

"Just trying to blend in." He made a show of turning so she could get a better view. She was stunning in the early afternoon light, though he did his best not to let his admiration of her show too much. It was obvious she did not trust him yet, and he planned to use this day as an opportunity for her to see his sincerity, and desperation for that matter, in asking for her help.

As if she had read his mind, she said, "If you're hoping I'll change my mind, you're in for disappointment." Shaye spun on her heel and joined the dancing townsfolk in the square. Brina shrugged her shoulders at him and followed her friend to join the festivities. A roguish-looking man with Skagan braids grabbed Shaye by the waist, turning her to the music. She welcomed the presence of the man, dancing closely with him like they were old friends. Sorin felt a tinge of jealousy. *This is going to be harder than I thought.*

Sorin waited until the song ended to approach them. "May I cut in?"

The Skagan looked at Sorin, as if sizing him up, before he spoke. "Man, she would eat you alive."

Sorin laughed, "Of that, I have no doubt."

Shaye shoved the Skagan in the shoulder playfully. "Haskell, this is..."

Sorin finished the lie for her: "Sir Sorin, pleasure to meet you." He shook Haskell's hand with a firm grip.

"Ah, one of the famous Mortal Knights I have heard so much about. My Captain was a member of the order, once upon a time. Tough bunch, the lot of you."

"We like to think so," Sorin joked.

Shaye interrupted, "I believe you were asking me to dance, Sir Sorin... Or would you two gentlemen prefer to dance together?"

Haskell patted her on the back. "Plenty of fire in this one."

"I've noticed." Sorin chuckled when Shaye shot a deadly warning glance in his direction.

Haskell didn't seem to catch the exchange as he excused himself, "Well I must be off. She is all yours, Sir Sorin. I'm off to find a bard and a brothel." As he strode away, he shouted back to Shaye, "Don't do anything I would do!"

Sorin took Shaye's hand in his and placed a hand on her waist. They moved off-beat to the music, and she laughed, "You're a terrible dancer!"

"I admit I'm a bit rusty, milady, but how can I be expected to follow the music when I'm so distracted by my beautiful dance partner?"

Shaye snorted, "You are a shameless flirt, King Sorin."

"Sorin. Just Sorin, please."

Shaye shook her head, but Sorin did not miss the smile on her face. "You are the strangest royal I have ever met."

"I'm just trying to do the right thing." He was sincere when he said it.

The sun caught Shaye's golden eyes, making them spark like fire. "I'm trying to believe that."

Before Sorin could respond, she pulled away, giving him a small curtsey, and turned to join Brina and her family at their stand. He had wanted to tell her to come with him so he could prove that his words were true. There was so much more that he wanted to tell her... About the night of the coup and how he had dreamed of her after; but that would have to wait. Once she agreed to come with them, then he would have his chance. *If* she agreed.

The festival went on well into the evening. He chatted with local fishermen and townsfolk, listening to the rumors circling the death of the King and the darkness pushing onto their shores. Their voices were filled with worry, some blamed the King for letting Magi stay in Asterion when they should have been exiled, while others spoke confidently of the capable lad who had taken the throne. They were sure that he would do his duty well and protect them as his father had. If only they knew how far in over his head he was.

No one recognized him, of course. He had spent most of his time as Prince training with Bron and the others or studying in the library. When given the chance, he would dress in clothing like the style he wore now and spend the day fishing or hunting. Walking around as the Prince of Asterion drew more attention than he liked, and, in his opinion, it was better to spend the day as just another man instead.

A few times throughout the day he had caught Shaye's eye, winking or smiling at her, and making her roll her eyes at his persistence. At one point he could have sworn she even made a vulgar gesture at him. She was bold and he admired a woman who wasn't intimidated by his status.

The day was growing cooler as night approached. Sorin was leaning against a brightly painted building, drink in hand. He watched as Bron and Anik gave children piggyback rides around a patch of grass nearby. The children were pretending to be knights while the men pretended to be their noble steeds. He laughed at the ridiculous sight of two of the most decorated knights in all Asterion galloping around.

Brina surprised Sorin at his side, offering a fresh berry tart. "Thank you." He gladly accepted the treat, even though he'd had his fill from the many different stands lined throughout the streets, selling fare from fish to pie.

"My dad made it. It's one of his specialties." She eyed Sorin, making him shift under her gaze. "Do you really need her?"

The boldness of her question caught him off guard. He had been around courtiers, who liked to dance around what they genuinely wanted to say, almost as if it were an art form, for far too long. He wanted to return her candor, so he answered honestly, "Aside from various advisors telling me that I do, there is definitely something in my gut that says the answer is 'yes.' We need her."

"Is your gut often right about these things?"

He chuckled, "You have no idea."

"She's been through hell. If she agrees to go with you and something happens to her—"

"I'll have you to answer to," he finished for her. "You and that axe of yours?"

"Exactly." She turned to walk away, taking the hand of a man who had been waiting for her. He handed her a beautiful purple flower and she blushed. Sorin watched them for a moment, noting how easily they talked to each other. They were so at ease with one another, the first signs of romance clear to anyone who looked at them. Sorin felt a tinge of jealousy again. This time the feeling came at the thought of having that sort of compatibility with someone. To be carefree and able to enjoy a festival without doom looming over them, was something he envied. Sorin sighed and finished his tart.

A while later he found himself surrounded by a group of older gentlemen, former soldiers from the old king's army. They swapped stories from their glory days and saluted each other, drunk from a day's worth of drinking. A few patted Sorin on the back, offering up a glass in cheers, which he returned halfheartedly.

Sorin humored them but he was distracted, searching the crowd for Shaye, when he heard a man grumble, "If I lose another coin to that girl, I won't be able to eat for the next week. She's damned lucky, that one." Two old timers were pouring themselves ale from a nearby barrel.

"Luck's got nothin' to do with it. She's one of them Magi that turned up after the uprising. Showed up in them woods just north of here, covered in blood. Rolland has always been too welcoming." He slurred his words, stumbling into one of the barrels. "Witches have no place here. Should have banished em' all to The Beyond." He took a long drink from his cup, spilling most of it into his filthy beard.

Sorin had heard talk like this often. There was still animosity between humans and Magi. Old prejudices lingered in the older generations, still hurt by the favor

Sorcerers and Mages used to enjoy. How easily had they forgotten that the Witches and lower Magi castes were suffering right alongside them during the old king's reign: paying hefty taxes, eating poor crops deemed unworthy of gracing noble plates, being subjected to the whims of the wealthy.

He followed the sound of men shouting and laughing. They were gathered in a tent, drunk on ale, and lost in a game of Passe-Dix, a popular dice game amongst the working class. In the middle of all the commotion, he was surprised to see Shaye, dice in hand and a pile of coins beside her. She really was taking them for all they had. And she seemed to be enjoying herself immensely.

The man in front of her was grumbling something about losing to a female. He stomped away with a pout. No one else seemed eager to lose their hard-earned wages to her tonight.

"Come on, who's up for another round?" She smiled slyly at the men around the table, candlelight shining on her. "I'll even triple the stakes." The flowers in her hair were gone and she had it up in a messy pile on her head, tied around with a strip of leather. He thought she could not possibly look more glorious than she did at that moment. Her golden eyes were glittering in the lantern light, her face aglow with the rush of winning.

"I'll give it a try." Sorin sat down across from her, propping his feet up on the table.

She snorted, "I would *love* to take your money." She grabbed a few coins, tossing them into the pot.

"Oh, I don't want to play for money."

Some men in the crowd hooted at the insinuation. Shaye scoffed and Sorin put his hands behind his head. She rolled the dice around in her hand, intrigue showed plainly on her face. "Is that so?" She cocked her head to the side playfully. "Tell me then, what is it that you have in mind, *Sorin*?" The way she said his name without his title made his pulse quicken. It was obvious she enjoyed taunting him.

"I win, and you come with us. No complaint, no argument. You come and you *help*."

"And if I win?" She leaned forward, the ties to her dress had started to come unlaced. He had a sneaking suspicion that she knew and had simply chosen to use it to her advantage. Perhaps she had not won that large pile of money by playing fair. He eyed the dice in her hand... Loaded. She *was* cheating.

He suppressed a smile. "I'll buy you a ship. You *are* in the trade business, are you not?" Judging from how well she held her own amongst these men and how she had stood her ground in front of Bron, he doubted she was an apprentice in the Guild, as her papers stated. But he decided to give her the courtesy of pretending. Whatever she had been doing up until this point was none of his business.

Her eyebrows went up at that. He had her attention now. Distant shouts came from the other side of the square, men deep in their cups, starting to fight.

"What good is a ship if I can't sail it on the strait?"

"That's a good point. Perhaps we should skip the roll and you should just agree to come anyway." Sorin grabbed the dice, tossing them up in his hand then catching them elegantly. "If you can help me set things right then there will be no danger to stop you from sailing, and I'll still give you a ship for your trouble. It's a win-win situation."

The crowd around them had begun to disperse, the men no longer interested in the stakes of Sorin and Shaye's game. But Sorin could tell that Shaye was weighing them in her mind. He knew he was one step closer to having her convinced, and he smiled, pleased with himself.

"I still need more time to think; but I'll admit, you may have yourself a deal. *Your Majesty*." They both rose to shake, just as a terrible rumble sounded through the square. Then the screaming began.

Sorin reached behind for his swords, then remembered with a start that he had left them in the old inn they had been staying at. Angry at his own foolishness, he looked around for Bron and his men. They must have had the same thoughts, as he spotted them grabbing anything nearby that could be used as a weapon.

Unsure of what had caused the commotion, Sorin turned to Shaye, "Stay here."

"Like hell!" Shaye shouted over the panicked cries of the townspeople. She pulled a knife from under her skirts. He looked at her in surprise, but she just shrugged, "What, a girl can't be prepared?"

Sorin would have laughed, had a piercing shriek not cut through the crowd. There was no doubt that whatever had crashed the festival was not of the human realm. "Stay close," he commanded her. If she was going to insist on going, then he'd at least have to keep her near enough to protect her, dagger, or no dagger.

Frightened people were running up from the docks, shoving past one another as they tried to escape the beast that had emerged from the water. Sorin and Shaye had to push their way through the crowd. Bron, Elijah, and Anik were closing in beside them, dodging terrified civilians.

Sorin shouted to them, "Any idea what that monstrosity is?" He pointed to the hideous, dragon-like creature ahead.

Shaye surprised him with the answer, "It's a *Cirein Croin*. They have not been seen on Asterion soil in nearly a century. It must have boarded a fisherman's ship. They have the ability to shapeshift into a smaller fish, allowing unsuspecting fishermen to bring them ashore, where they then shift back, in order to feed." Sweat was already beading on her forehead.

It was hard to believe that this gigantic creature had come

aboard one of the tiny fisherman hauls. Either way, they had to stop it from causing any more harm. By the time they reached the dock, the ground was wet, drenched in water and blood. The Cirein Croin hissed and shrieked at the sight of them, ready to feast some more.

"Any idea on how we kill it?" he asked Shaye sincerely.

"Same way you kill any other fish, I suppose."

"Great."

Bron and Elijah had disappeared from his view; he knew they would be trying to find a way from behind. They needed to surround the water dragon and ambush it. Anik came around a few feet from Sorin and Shaye, green with disgust. Shaye gripped her knife and bounced on her feet. This was clearly not her first time in a fight.

Sorin grabbed a nearby fishing spear and bounded for the monster before it had a chance to lunge at him first. It took the hit from him with a wild buck, shrieking in pain, but it did not stop. Its slimy head slammed into Sorin, sending him flying into the water. He struggled to come up for air, his boots weighing him down. He kicked them off, dragging himself quickly to shore. He spat the salty water out and shook his head, trying to regain his bearings. From the water, he could see Bron and his men on the beast, doing their best to overpower it. It was relentless.

When Sorin made it to land, he began looking wildly around for anything to use as a weapon now that his spear was uselessly sticking out of the beast's neck. He scrambled for rope hanging on one of the boats and secured it into a loop. He had roped horses and cattle before when they had visited the farms in Norbrach, but he had never tried his luck on a magical dragon fish.

Here goes nothing, he thought, as he swung and missed twice before landing his mark. He pulled with every ounce of strength he could muster, his bare feet sliding on the rough, wet ground.

Between the rope pulling around its neck and the hits the monster was taking from the three knights, it went down with an earth-shattering thud. In the blink of an eye Sorin watched as Shaye took an oar, cracking it hard across the beast's head. It went still from the blow. Both Sorin and Shaye turned away as Bron cut the head from its body, a necessary safety measure, but a gruesome one all the same.

Shaye turned to him. Sorin could see the adrenaline and relief coursing through her eyes, her hair aglow beneath the moonlight. Crying cut through his thoughts as he looked around at the destruction the monster had left in its wake. Panic hit him like a storm when he saw the source of the cries.

A few townspeople stood around the battered docks. To one side of him, a distraught woman was wailing for her husband. A young boy, no older than fifteen, stood quiet, tears streaming down his bloodstained face. And *Brina*.

Brina was lying in a pool of blood. Sorin could not tell if it belonged to her or the man that she held onto. His heart sank when he realized it was the man from earlier. The one who had brought her the flower. She was screaming for Shaye, and he watched in terror as Shaye ran toward them. The look of triumph on her face at having defeated the beast was now replaced with cold hard fear. She knelt next to her friend, searching Brina for any sign of injury.

When Sorin joined them, he noted that Brina seemed to only have a few superficial cuts and scrapes along her face and arms. He called out for someone to get a healer. Shaye was busy fussing over a sobbing Brina when Sorin noticed the man's injuries. His head was in Brina's lap, and she was pressing down on a wound beneath his torn and bloodied shirt.

He nudged Shaye and nodded toward the man. The man,

unconscious now from the pain, had taken a devastating bite from the water dragon. Shaye put a hand to her mouth, and Sorin steadied her by placing his hand on her shoulder. Brina was begging the man, Leif, to wake up. Tears fell down her bruised face as she pleaded with them, "He saved me, Shaye, he saved me. Please don't let him die." Shaye looked utterly helpless as she sat in the pool of blood next to her friend.

Anik arrived a moment later with the town doctor. The man wasted no time going to work on Leif, doing his best to stop the wounds from bleeding, but it was no use. The attack on him was fatal and all they could do now was sit quietly while Brina said goodbye.

CHAPTER TWELVE

Sorin

Once the doctor had declared Leif dead, they gathered up his body and the body of the sea monster's other victims. Some people were still considered missing as they had not found their bodies yet, but Sorin could see that no one held any hope of their recovery. The festival had been shut down the following day and funerals had been planned in haste.

The next afternoon, Shaye and Sorin accompanied a grief-stricken Brina to the home of Leif's family. His mother and sisters were dressed for mourning, with black lace and veils covering their faces. Leif's father, a gentle man with a quiet demeanor, was accepting condolences in the hall as people filed in one by one to pay their respects.

Sorin felt out of place here; these people had known Leif since he was a babe. There was a strong sense of community, and he envied the warmth with which they talked to one another. He stood quietly in the corner of the small town-home, unsure of what he could do to help this heartbroken family.

Shaye had not asked him to come, but she also had not protested when he showed up at her doorstep to escort her to the funeral. When he offered his arm to her she had taken it, holding onto it tightly as they made their way through town. The ceremony had been nice enough, sending Leif off to The Mother from whom they all came before birth. His sisters had thrown petals in his wake as men from town carried his shrouded body, placing it gently on the funeral pyre. His father set fire to it while a local priestess honored Leif with the ancient rites. She stood near the pyre in a simple white gown, calling on the Fates to carry Leif's spirit through the smoke and to the paradise which lays beyond life.

Sorin had desperately wanted to reach for Shaye's hand while silent tears streamed down her face, but he had resisted. She had done her best all day to stay strong for her friend, who was grieving the hardest. It had turned out that the scene Sorin had witnessed at the festival was the moment Leif had asked for her hand in marriage. He had given her the flower with a ring tied to it. She had said yes, and they had gone down to the docks for privacy while they celebrated. Brina blamed herself for the loss of her love, but Sorin knew it was his fault. It was his fault for not taking the reports more seriously, for not putting a defense on their shores sooner.

Shaye wandered through the people crowded inside the modest home and to his side, handing him a plate of food. Her eyes were red around the edges, but she was holding herself together. Sorin wished he could tell her that it was okay for her to be sad, that she did not have to try to hide her feelings around him or anyone else. But he held his tongue, accepting the heaping pile of food.

"Thank you. You didn't have to go through the trouble."

"Well, if you're going to hide in the corner all day, then you should at least eat. It would be embarrassing if you passed out in front of the whole town." She joked, but the laughter was gone from her voice. She just sounded tired.

"Did you sleep at all?"

"Not much." She hesitated before she admitted, "I have trouble sleeping most nights. Last night's events stirred up some old memories that I couldn't shake." She added unconvincingly, "I'll be fine."

"I'm trying to make up for it, you know."

Shaye looked at him, puzzled. "Make up for what exactly?"

"My father's sins. Those are the memories you are referring to, are they not?"

At that, she simply nodded. It looked as if she was about to say something when a commotion came from the hall. They could hear shouting as the funeral guests crowded around the foyer. Sorin pushed through the crowd, Shaye trailing closely behind him.

One of the men from town was shouting at a small woman who had walked in alone. "You have no business being here, Witch."

"I've only come to pay my respects." The woman was around his mother's age, with the tanned skin of someone who spent their days outside. "Liza, you know me, I only want to pay my respects to you and your boy." The woman extended a hand to Leif's mother, Liza, who stood wide eyed, seemingly unsure of what to do or say.

Sorin reached out a hand to stop Shaye from getting involved, but he was not fast enough. Shaye was between the woman and the man blocking the Witch's path into the house in a matter of seconds. She too was Magi, and he worried they would turn on her if she got in the middle of the disagreement.

Another woman chimed in, "Magi are not welcome here. Look at what magic does." She pointed to Leif's family.

More people joined in, telling the woman to leave. The

situation was getting ugly, and it was happening extremely fast. Shaye went to the Magi woman and whisper something in her ear. The woman nodded, wiping tears from her eyes. She patted Shaye on the hand, giving her a small, sad smile. Before she turned to leave, she looked at Leif's mother and held a hand to her heart. Then she was gone.

Shaye looked hurt and exhausted; Sorin was not sure what she had said to the woman, but it had worked to deescalate the situation. Sorin was shaken by the scene he had witnessed; he had not expected things to turn so quickly. He could see that the people of Asterion needed someone to blame for the tragedy they had witnessed. Fear was a dangerous thing, more dangerous than any magical monster. If they believed the Magi in town held any bit of responsibility for what was happening, then things were about to get incredibly bad.

They stayed throughout the day, saying their goodbyes at nightfall. Sorin walked Brina and Shaye back to the inn. He lingered on the porch while Shaye went in to see Brina off to bed. Sorin waited with a potent glass of wine that Rolland had brought him. He was alone on the porch of the *Brass Blossom*, watching townspeople heading home for the night. Some spoke of the tragedy on the docks, others were too drunk to talk at all.

A soft sea breeze blew at his hair, and he closed his eyes, taking it in. Aramoor was his favorite city in all of Asterion. The architecture throughout the city was astounding and ahead of its time. Colorful townhomes stood tall, lining the clean cobblestone streets. Trade had been doing well before the blight and the Guilds did well to distribute that wealth throughout Aramoor. They took care of schools for young children as well as trade schools for anyone looking to join the Guilds as an apprentice. Sorin had often thought how he would have liked to have been a fisherman, if he had been born into another life.

His mother had taken him into the city often, even well after his family had taken the throne. She had wanted him to know the people, to know what they liked and what they needed in life. "It is the key to a successful Asterion," she had said to him. Sorin knew she was right, but he had often wondered about the Magi in Asterion. Who was looking out for their needs? Of course, they were offered a place in the new world, but were they genuinely happy? Sorin thought of Shaye and how her hands had shaken when he had first arrived. He wondered what would make *her* happy. The thought surprised him, and he opened his eyes.

Shaye came out and leaned against the side of the building, arms crossed in front of her. Her hair was a wild mess of tangles, and she still wore the black dress she had borrowed from Brina. Sorin offered her the jacket that Rolland had lent him, but she politely refused.

"I know you don't want to hear this, but time isn't on our side Shaye, so I have to ask... Do you see now? This threat is real, and we need your help. Even if there is only the slightest chance that you are indeed capable of what we hope, it is worth trying. What happened down at the docks is only the beginning." He shivered, the night air was cool on his skin and the sight of Leif laying on the ground in a pool of blood clouded his memory.

After Leif's death, most of the townspeople had cleared out by the time Sorin had left the docks. He had sent a guard to the palace with a signed account of the night's events, ordering General Tyrell to post troops along the harbour. It was their best defense right now.

Shaye hung her head and furrowed her brow. "I know helping is the right thing to do. But I cannot forget, nor can I forgive, the past." When she looked back up at him, he felt the fire of her words. He understood her position, and did not judge her for it, but it did not change the fact that he needed her.

"I can see that you struggle with your past. Your family lost everything that night, but you have a family here and now; a *human* family that does not stand a chance against the creatures reaching our shore. Even with the guards I have ordered here, it may not be enough. Wouldn't you do anything to protect them?"

"Of course I would. I would go to the ends of the world."

"Then do just *that*. Go north with me. Trouble has arrived in *your* backyard; this is not something we can dismiss as rumor anymore. This time it was Leif, next it could be Brina. Help your family by helping me." As much as he knew they both wanted to turn away from the responsibility, he was speaking the truth.

Shaye stood tall and faced him. She looked as fierce as any knight he had ever seen. There was not one ounce of weakness in her voice when she said, "Tell me what I have to do."

CHAPTER THIRTEEN

Shaye

They left at first light, just as the sun began to peek out from behind the brightly painted houses leading down to the water. Shaye had sent word to Haskell, letting him know that she was heading north with a friend. It was a vague note, but she was unsure of what else she could say. She still could not quite believe she had agreed to go.

As Sorin and his men readied the horses, she bid a teary-eyed farewell to the Erland family, assuring them that she would return home safely. Hugging Brina in the threshold of the comfortable inn she had come to call home, she joked, "Just another grand adventure for the books."

Brina did not return the smile. Dark circles gave away the fact that she had not slept at all the night before. Shaye had stayed up with her late into the night, talking about Leif and their childhood memories of him. Brina explained how their romance had begun and how he would leave little presents for her to find around the inn.

Shaye wanted to kick herself for not knowing more about what had been going on in her friend's life, to have not known that she had been in love with that silly boy down the street that they had teased relentlessly. And worse, for not being able to save him. Shaye would spend the rest of her days trying to make that up to Brina. That night had been the first time in her life that she desperately wished she had control of her magic. All of that would change now, as she was determined not to stand by powerless ever again.

Rolland and Rebecca had smiled at her, wiping the tears from her cheeks. This goodbye felt much heavier than the other times she had left home. A new burden rested on her shoulders, accompanied by a hint of guilt. It felt like a betrayal to her people that she had just agreed to help a man whose father had taken their Mother-given magic from them. The man who was responsible for her nightmares. As much as she wanted to believe that Sorin was not like his father, he was still a stranger to her.

Once on Finn, Shaye turned to look back one last time at the peaceful cobblestone roads of Aramoor. The rising sun sparkled on the horizon of the sea; she hoped this would not be the last time she laid eyes on it.

They rode hard and fast throughout the rest of the day, stopping only to water and rest the horses. Hours passed, and once the sun had set, Sorin announced that they would stop for camp. They found a safe place to make camp off one of the popular routes to the North. The route they were following consisted of dense woods and rolling farmland, and showed no signs of trouble.

The men scouted the area and settled their camp into a small copse of trees, giving them enough cover for the night. Around the fire they feasted on the meal Rolland had sent them off with: smoked venison, seasoned in rich herbs from Sagon. Herbs that would soon be hard to come by if the trade strait did not open back up. Shaye grabbed another slice of buttered bread and watched Sorin across the fire. From the moment they had dismounted from the horses, he'd had his nose buried in a dusty old book titled, *The Final Judgment.* Shaye eyed the dusty book that was peeling at the edges, from where she sat on her bedroll.

Her butt ached from riding in the saddle for so long. She was used to being at sea and not on her horse for such long periods of time. Even Finn was crankier than usual, snapping at the other horses when they came too close. She stretched her legs out, reaching to touch her toes.

"Looks ominous," Shaye called to Sorin, interrupting his reading. The firelight danced on his face like little creatures of light. He looked startled, like he had forgotten anyone else was there. Bron was spread out on a bedroll not far from Sorin, looking up at the night sky and humming an old ballad Shaye had heard often in the taverns.

"It is." He cleared his throat and read out loud, "*In a time after creation, following the great war in The Beyond, three Magi brothers were tested. They were granted objects of powerful magic—each a test of their true nature and ability to forgive.*" Shaye and the men around the fire listened intently as he went on, "*The first brother, Leto, was gifted a stave to amplify his power. The second brother, Roth, was granted a gilded sword, powerful enough to cut down any threat he faced. And the third, Pris, was given an obsidian pendant to protect him from harm.*

These brothers had witnessed the fall of their country, and to rebuild their forces and exact revenge, had ventured south to a new land. The Mother found them and blessed them with these objects, granting them her favor and the opportunity for a fresh start. But no magic can be wielded without sacrifice. Their sacrifice would come in the form of a test: that test was forgiveness. To determine whether they were worthy of such power, they would have to give up their thirst for vengeance, or prove their unworthiness by seeking out those who had wronged them." Shaye shivered despite the heat from the fire, as Sorin continued to read.

"The first brother used his chance to forgive and find love. Leto hid away his stave and was rewarded with a companion. The second brother put away past grievances, throwing the sword into the abyss, and was rewarded with peace. Driven by such hate, the third brother was unable to let go. He chose vengeance and a river of blood was spilled. As a result, his object was cursed and lost to the world, destined to spread greed and destruction." Sorin closed the book and looked into Shaye's eyes. The fire dimmed before them, almost as if it too, were disturbed by the tale.

Shaye was the first to break the silence. "The relic... You believe it's one of the objects in the story?" It was a definite possibility. In a world that once held infinite magic, it was hard to discount the theory that these magical objects would have been created centuries ago.

"I do. My father never spoke of the relic he used to suppress the magic here. He did not want to risk anyone tracking it down. But he had me study these texts front to back since I was a child. I always thought it was to keep me busy, but I think he was trying to tell me something, in case anything ever went wrong. The Stave had the ability to amplify power. What if it can also dampen it?"

Shaye thought for a moment. This story was the only clue as to what the relic was and where it had come from. Any lead was a good lead at this point. She picked at a patch of green grass beside her.

"How will you know where to look for it?"

Sorin smiled wickedly at her. "Let's just say an old friend of the family is about to owe me a favor."

Later, once the fire had died down again, Shaye laid on her bundle of blankets, looking up at the stars. The further they traveled, the brighter the stars seemed to shine. It was something she had ached for while living in the East. Here in Asterion the stars seemed to reach for you, bright and hopeful. The night sky always shined brighter under their light, casting shades of deep blue and purple in the darkness. It was like its own sort of magic. A magic it had held onto no matter what Asterion faced over the ages. She found herself excited to see that sky again; there was *nothing* in this world whose beauty compared to the Northern Lights.

It had been a long time since she had been this far north. She had left the Guild to escape Asterion and the ghosts that haunted her there. And now she had a nagging sense that these ghosts would be making their presence felt more and more, the closer she came to Brenmar and the Winter Palace.

That night, she dreamed of darkness again. She was lost in a vast *nothingness*. From inside that darkness a voice called to her, familiar and warm. *Shaye.* No matter how hard she tried, she could not reach it. She tried to go to it, but the darkness swallowed her up and she awoke to the smoke of their dying campfire and the snores of the men around her.

"Shaye," Sorin whispered from the across the firepit. "Are you alright?"

"I'm fine. Sorry to wake you."

"I was having trouble sleeping anyway."

Shaye heard rustling and could see Sorin moving around. He came to her side with his bedroll and laid it an arm's length away from her. She tried to stop him, "Oh, you don't have to..."

He swatted a hand in the air. "Nonsense, I should have known better than to sleep too close to Bron. He snores like an Ogre."

Shaye laughed and did not argue further. She laid back, staring up at the night sky trying to will herself back to sleep. Sorin shifted around on his bedroll and turned to her. "I have them too, you know? The dreams..."

Shaye rolled to face him. "How to you deal with them?"

"I focus on what is happening in the present. Sometimes it works and other times it doesn't."

Shaye laughed. "The only thing that's ever helped me is running far from this place."

"Then why return?"

"Fate."

They did not speak again and soon Shaye drifted off to sleep to the sound of Sorin breathing beside her. She had done as he suggested and focused on the present; on the intriguing man beside her. For the remainder of the night, her nightmares kept at bay.

She did not mention her dreams to the rest of her travel companions. They were just learning to trust one another, and she did not think it necessary to let them see how scared she was inside. Over the next couple of days, they traveled mostly in silence. Sorin and the others were on edge, listening for any sign of danger and looking for anything out of sorts. Things grew more tense as they traveled further north. They stopped running into travelers on the road, and the atmosphere seemed to change the closer they got to the villages in Norbrach. Shaye knew with the events of the Spring festival coming to an end, there should be more people around, but it seemed they had not yet returned.

Although their days were fueled with a quiet air, each night the men would drink and sing. They would sing of places they had been and the women they had met (even bedded) along the way. Shaye knew too well of the need for reprieve from a long days' worth of travel.

On the night before they were to reach Norbrach, Sorin braved a question Shaye had been expecting him to ask. He had laid his bedroll out near hers, something he had taken to doing since that first night. The others were distracted with a game of cards when Sorin grinned at her and, leaning in, asked, "You're not really an apprentice in the Guild, are you?"

She scoffed at him, "What makes you say that?"

"The way you carry yourself. It's hard to imagine you

taking orders from a pompous merchant. And I've seen the company you keep. You expect me to believe that Haskell is also a merchant?" He winked at her, and she noticed a small dimple in his cheek when he smiled.

Shaye gave in and told him about the crew she had spent the last few months traveling with. The ship was captained by a former privateer, Captain Thorsten. Sorin's face lit up at the name. "I've heard of him. He was quite successful during the war between Sagon and Morvak. And before that, was a renowned knight in my father's army."

Shaye nodded. "Yes, the man is a legend. And when I found myself out of work, they offered me a place on their crew and welcomed me into their fold. Traveling with you and your men actually reminds me a bit of those nights on the ship." She eyed him warily, waiting for his reaction. "You're not going to have me arrested for it are you?"

"Of course not. However, I will use my position as your King to order you to get some rest. Your training begins at first light." He laid back, folding his arms behind his head and shutting his eyes.

Shaye spent the rest of the night aware of how close he was to her. She was becoming alarmingly comfortable around him, and though she did not want to admit it to him, she was enjoying his company. She could hear his steady breath and sense the warmth of him. That night, she slept peacefully with no nightmares to haunt her.

Sorin stayed true to his word. The moment she opened her eyes in the morning he handed her a pile of books and insisted on her reading up on basic Magi practices. Every time they stopped to rest and water the horses, Sorin would push for her to try her hand at spells and enchantments. She failed each time, but continued to try anyway.

"It's no use." Shaye threw the book Sorin had handed her early that morning. "I can't feel anything. Cannot conjure any sliver of power. All I seem to be able to stir up is a pounding headache."

"Keep trying." It was always Sorin's answer when she wanted to stop. He was being a real pain in her ass. Her body ached from the ride, and they were running low on the food Rolland had sent them off with. She was hungry and tired and in no mood for his encouraging smiles.

"I *am* trying. I have been trying all day. We're nearly to Norbrach and I still can't do even the most elementary level of spells." She ran a hand through her hair and looked up at the clear blue sky. She was frustrated and exhausted from trying and failing.

"You're not trying hard enough." Sorin pushed, "You need to let go of whatever it is that's holding you back. You're *scared*."

Before she could stop herself, Shaye's temper flared, and she felt heat rising from within her. *Scared? How dare he accuse me of being scared. He is the one who asked for my help. I told him I had no power to tap into.* She'd had enough of his pushing. Of his sympathetic glances and encouraging words. She was sick of riding and of sleeping on the hard ground. Tired of reading and remembering. Worst of all, she was exhausted from the constant fear that the nightmares would return. Something told her the respite would not last, they always returned.

Fed up with it all, with this entire situation she had gotten herself into, she acted before she could stop herself. She kicked out a leg, sweeping Sorin off his feet in one swift movement. He hit the dusty ground with a thud, stopping Bron and the others in their tracks.

They were too stunned to react as Sorin rolled himself out of her reach. But she did not stop; lashing out felt too good. She threw a punch that connected to his shoulder. This time he reacted. He grabbed her arm before she could swing again. But when she looked up at his face, she did not see anger as she had expected. Instead, he was smiling at her. There was surprise in his eyes, but he was almost grinning.

"You think this is funny?" She demanded, feeling more irritation rise from inside her. *Why isn't he mad? Why is he just standing there taking the brunt of my frustration?*

"I think you're finally letting go." He still held onto her arm, pulling her closer to him. He was serious now. "Let go of that fear. Embrace those feelings of frustration and admit to yourself that you are angry. Angry with me. With life. With everyone who has ever let you down or hurt you."

She paused at the truth in his words. She could pretend that she was fine, keep the nightmares to herself; but the truth of the matter was that she had never felt more helpless and lost.

She took a moment to catch her breath before what she had just done registered in her mind. She suddenly felt very aware of her body, so close to his. *By The Mother. I just hit the King.* Sorin loosened his grip on her. She was appalled as she stepped back away from him. She looked at Bron and the other men, still standing there, looking at their king, wide-eyed.

"We should keep going." Sorin gestured to the horses. "And Shaye, you're going to want to save some of that aggression for what we're about to do."

Shaye nodded, unable to meet his eyes. "Yes, Your Majesty."

CHAPTER FOURTEEN

Shaye

It was *mid-afternoon* when they reached the small village just north of Norbrach. The villages surrounding this area were some of the most prosperous areas in Asterion. Shaye had heard reports from Rolland that their friends who resided here had been experiencing a successful start to the season. From the looks of it, that was no longer the case; the crops looked as if they had died the moment they had sprouted. Anything that had grown had not survived, leaving rot on the ground. Although the weather had been agreeable at the start of the spring season, offering plenty of rain, the fields now looked as if they had suffered a drought.

The sight in the village was just as shocking. Carts had been left abandoned on the wide dirt road and houses were boarded shut. Shaye was not sure if families here had left because of the rumors or if they had experienced magical sightings firsthand. Regardless of why they had left, barren fields and missing farmers made Asterion vulnerable.

Shaye watched Sorin. She felt terrible for how she had behaved earlier, but was too embarrassed to bring it up. He was scanning the area with a sad look on his handsome face. Shaye clicked at Finn, bringing him up alongside Sorin's horse. "Are you okay?"

He paused before answering her. "With trade routes closed, the entire continent will be relying on crops and livestock provided by the farmers in this part of the territory. Without them, we have a nation on the brink of starvation."

Shaye didn't know what to say; it was one thing to hear about the state of things touched by the blight, but it was another to experience them firsthand. *This is just the start*; Shaye contemplated the state of things as she dismounted from Finn. He danced around anxiously, not wanting to be here anymore than she did.

She tried to lighten the mood. "Are you going to share with the class what we're doing here, Your Majesty?"

The men dismounted and Elijah led the horses to a nearby post. Bron drew his massive sword from its sheath and answered for Sorin. "We're here to hunt a monster." He bared his teeth in anticipation.

"And I suppose you, *oh gallant Mortal Knight*, are going to be the one to slay the beast," Shaye joked.

"It's only fair, since you got the last one." He nudged her in the side, nearly knocking her over from his size.

She shouted as he walked away, "That one was a team effort! You're just lucky Asterion craftsmen carve such sturdy oars!" He laughed, throwing a hand in the air as he dismissed her jest.

There was a crash from one of the nearby houses and Sorin held a finger to his lips. A memory flashed in her mind of a boy gripping her hand and holding a finger to his lips beneath the shadows of a stairwell. She shook the thought away, pulling the dagger from her belt. She was grateful to be wearing pants instead of a dress this time.

They stalked silently toward the sound. The hair on her

arms stood on end as a snarl vibrated from behind the house. From the sound of it, something was feeding. They were only a few paces away when it stopped.

Bile rose in her throat as a grotesque, fanged creature rounded the corner of one of the cottages. Its mouth was foaming and red, and its beady eyes squinted in the sunlight. The beast towered over them, taller than even Bron.

The Mortal Knight did not balk in the creature's presence. "Hope you practiced your enchantments today, milady."

She knew he had seen her practicing and failing spectacularly. She held back a retort as Bron's face lit up. Clearly in his element now, he and the others had chosen to don their armor this morning and now she knew why. She suddenly felt vulnerable in her plain leather jerkin, wishing she had her own set of armor.

"Here we go!" Bron shouted, and with a war cry he spun his broad sword until it was poised in front of him.

The creature roared and beelined for them, making all five of them scatter. It looked around, confused as to who it should go after, but it did not take long before it decided Bron would be the biggest threat out of all of them. It moved in on him with surprising speed considering how large it was.

Shaye recognized the magical creature from books she had read in the palace as a child. *Orcs* were humanoid monsters who, according to legend, were not the smartest creatures. They were a brutish type of Goblin, one that Shaye had been glad she'd never had the displeasure of crossing paths with before.

Bron and the beast clashed against one another, brute strength against brute strength. Bron smashed an elbow into the monster's face, dazing it long enough to come down with his great sword. The beast wailed at the contact, but did not go down. Sorin withdrew a sword from the baldrick on his back and jumped the creature from behind.

Shaye watched them fight the Orc with fierce determination for what felt like a lifetime. She looked at the other two knights, Elijah and Anik, wondering why they were just standing there beside her. "Shouldn't you do something to help them?"

They were leaning casually against a fence post. "Nah, it's good for them to struggle sometimes. Keeps 'em humble." Elijah winked at her and went back to watching his friends battle the beast.

At last, the monster fell to the ground long enough for Bron to run it through. Shaye cringed at the sight of it; when Anik noticed, he attempted to comfort her, "Orcs are notorious for cannibalism. Reports told us this one had killed a family of three in this village before turning on its own kind and eating them as well. Save your sympathies if you can."

With the beast defeated, Bron and Sorin took the time to wash up before they got back on the road. Shaye fed the horses, and noticed Elijah and Anik grabbing the Orc's body, rope in hand. She looked at them with bewilderment. They could not possibly be doing what she thought they were.

She shouted for Sorin when she realized they were bringing the beast with them. "Are you insane?" She rounded on him as they strapped its massive body to Bron's war horse.

"I know, listen, it's not something I'm happy to do, but we need it to make a deal with a Witch. *This* is the sort of payment she takes." He gestured to the creature, then helped Shaye mount Finn.

"This is wrong, Sorin. You are a *king*, not a bounty hunter." Shaye blocked his way with her horse. For the first time since they had met, Sorin actually looked annoyed with her.

"I'm doing what I must. The beast's death was swift and well deserved. He will not be able to harm anyone again. Honestly, will *nothing* ever please you?" He veered his horse around hers, continuing on his way.

Shaye huffed and shouted at his back, "Nothing *you* do!"

They rode in silence after that. Finn danced around with adrenaline from the danger he had felt during the fight. Shaye patted his neck and whispered to him, "I know, I know. *What have I gotten us into?*" He nodded his head as if agreeing with her and they were off again. This time to track down a Witch.

CHAPTER FIFTEEN

Sorin

The Hedge Witch lived alone in a wooded area just south of Brenmar. It was less than a day's ride to her cottage, and the smell wafting from the Orc was almost unbearable by the time they reached it. The riders all covered their faces with whatever they had been able to find, but even then, they could not mask the stench. It was making the horses restless, too. The heat from the springtime sunshine did not help, even with the slight breeze gracing the air.

Relief washed over him when they finally reached the Witch's land. Shaye had given Sorin the cold shoulder the entire way there. Not that he could blame her, he did not like what they were about to do any more than she did. The thought of her being angry with him was an unpleasant one.

Bron pulled his horse up beside him. "She'll get over it."

"She shouldn't have to. This is a nasty business."

"It bothers you, doesn't it?"

"Of course. What man in his right mind would want to ride through the woods with a carcass?"

"Not the Orc... her." Bron nodded his head toward Shaye,

who was just out of earshot. When Sorin failed to reply, Bron laughed, "It does! Oh man, I knew you liked her, but I didn't realize you *liked* her!"

"I have no idea what you're talking about." Sorin did his best to play it off.

Bron did not relent. "Sorin, we've been friends all our lives and I know you better than you know yourself. You have feelings for that woman, even if you're not ready to admit it to yourself."

Bron walked on ahead, leaving Sorin to sit in silence. Bron was right, but his feelings weren't important; there were more pressing things on the line than his heart.

They stopped at the edge of the Witch's land. Her cottage was quaint, the sort of place one would move to if they wanted isolation and privacy. A little garden surrounded the house, full of flowers and vegetables native to Asterion as well as some that he did not recognize. Clearly her little spot of land was immune to the strife the surrounding land was experiencing.

"Wait here." He motioned for the others to hold back as he dismounted and approached the Witch's dwelling. Hedge Witches had been considered the lowest caste of Magi before the uprising; and afterwards, a few of them had fled Asterion. He did not blame them, there was nothing left for them here.

According to his mother, Atropani was not a common Hedge Witch though. She was what they had labeled an *ancient*. One of the Witches who had perfected longevity and had lived for centuries. How she did this was a mystery and, honestly, he was not sure he wanted to know. But if anyone had an idea of where a long-lost relic had been hidden, it would be her.

Sorin knocked on the old wooden door, watching it open with a creak, exposing a humble-looking home. It was made up of only one room, with a loft for sleeping. It was hard to make out any furniture as his eyes adjusted to the darkness. From the doorway, he could not see anyone there. He took a deep breath, thinking he would be kicking himself later for this, and walked inside. The door shut behind him, making him jump in alarm. He really wished he had not left his weapons with the others outside.

The little cottage smelled of dead flowers, and the shades were drawn, making it difficult to see. And a fire crackled in the hearth. Approaching slowly, he noticed a woman sitting in the chair beside it. She was rocking back and forth and humming the same song Bron and Elijah had been singing earlier on the road.

The rocking stopped. "King Sorin." She had a voice like gravel, as if it had been an exceedingly long time since she last used it. "I wondered when you would be gracing my humble abode with your presence."

"You knew I would come." It was more a statement than a question. His mother had told him things about Atropani. She was the woman who had told his father where to find the relic all those years ago. He was not sure why, but this woman had single-handedly aided in the abolishment of magic, somehow keeping hers in the process. *Convenient*, Sorin thought.

When she stood, Sorin stumbled back into a nearby chair, knocking a dusty quilt to the ground. She was tall and, for lack of a better word, *ancient*; her gray-white hair was spun like cobwebs and her face was sunken in. Most shocking were the hollowed holes where her eyes should have been. Something his mother had failed to warn him about. Her appearance was shocking.

She laughed with a dry crackle, like bones under pressure, "Do not worry, boy. I am not going to hurt you. I am far too tired for that. Now, from the smell of you, you've brought me a gift."

"Not a gift. I am here to ask for a fair trade. The monster from Norbrach, an Orc, in exchange for information."

"I have a wealth of information, child. And I am happy to give it to you in exchange for the beast's body. But I think we'd better invite your friends in. I sense they're growing anxious at your absence." She held out a bone thin hand and the door opened, spilling Shaye and the others into the doorway, leaving them in a toppled heap. Sorin shook his head. They needed to work on following orders.

The Witch invited Shaye in, while Bron and Anik fetched the Orc's corpse for her. She began rummaging around her cupboards in search of something. What appeared to be used as the kitchen area was a jumble of jars, old ingredients, and an alarming number of knives. The cupboards contained empty jars as well as some filled with strange liquids and crushed herbs. How she could find anything in the mass of different herbs and potions, he had no idea, but she managed fine.

With an old stone pestle, she began grinding ingredients together in a bowl, leaving Shaye and Sorin to sit on two small stools, unsure of what they should do or say next. The old Witch spoke, "You're here for the relic."

Sorin nodded and Shaye elbowed him in the side. *Shit. Atropani's eyes,* he felt like an idiot. "Y-yes, we would like any information you have on its whereabouts." Atropani had him on edge; she looked as he imagined death itself would look in corporeal form. He needed to gather his thoughts so they could get the information and leave. He did not want to spend any more time here than he had to.

"Oh, I've got information. I am what you would call a *seer.*" She faced Shaye and smiled, "I do not need my eyes to see, for I already know all that has passed." She tapped a long, thin finger to her head and sat down. Sorin noticed a spider crawling on her shoulder and shivered.

The sooner they got out of there the better. "Please, Atropani, my mother assured me you would help us." There was a thud at the door as Bron and Anik brought the creature inside, struggling to fit it through.

"I remember your mother fondly. A strong woman, that one. Much like the woman sitting at your side now." A faint smile spread across her cracked lips. "I will honor my end of the trade, King Sorin, but I will not take sides." She gestured for the knights to set the Orc on the long dinner table near where they sat. Elijah gagged beside them, doing his best to keep his breakfast down.

Atropani continued, "*Help*, I cannot give. I am simply an observer of histories. You see, my sisters and I have been here far longer than you, than even the relic itself." She smiled, revealing rotting teeth.

Recognition lit up on Shaye's face as she blurted, "The Fates."

"Clever child. Yes, most call us Fates, but The Mother called us *Moirai*. We were here at creation, gifted the ability only to observe, never to live. Never married and unable to bear children. Sentenced to be the watchers of humanity. I have witnessed wars and curses, families of power rising and falling, I have seen kings executed, and kings taken by sickness." Sorin felt a stab of grief at her last words.

He understood now. "You are the Moirai of the past, then. And your sisters..."

"Clothsari, the present, and Lachtori, the future. You are correct."

Sorin looked to Shaye, whose face was a mixture of astonishment and nerves as she spoke, "I heard stories as a child but never imagined you'd be *here*. All this time."

"Best to hide in plain sight, my dear." Atropani crept slowly up to the Orc, and to Sorin's horror, picked up a hatchet, cutting its hand off. Elijah could not hold back now;

he ran out the door, the sounds of heaving outside disrupting the quiet disgust of the rest of the room.

Atropani ignored them and did not miss a beat as she took the severed hand to the kitchen and began working on some sort of potion.

They were getting nowhere. The sun was beginning to set, and they were wasting time here. "Please, will you tell us where it is?"

"You are on the right track, for it is where this all began. Follow the northern stars; they will take you to my sister, gifted with the sight of the present. She will guide you the rest of the way. We have been expecting you for some time now. But beware, for creatures in the past have risked their lives protecting what you seek... For the Stave of Leto was never meant for mortal hands."

The Stave. Sorin had been right. That was the relic they were searching for. "Thank you." He rose to leave, motioning for Shaye to follow. He paused to ask something he had been wondering the entire ride there. "Atropani, why did you help my father acquire the Stave? Knowing what he would use it for."

"I wondered when you would ask." She wheezed as she sighed, "Long ago, I knew a girl. She was born of darkness, a daughter of Obsidian. It broke my heart to see how she struggled with her demons, knowing I could not do more to help her. I chose to honor her memory by aiding your father. With the Stave under his control, I had hoped it would not fall into the hands of the same darkness that claimed her all those ages ago."

Sorin nodded in understanding and turned to leave, no intention of ever stepping foot in the seer's home again, if he could help it.

"May The Mother bless you, King Sorin. For when it comes to Her, there is always more to it. The idea of destiny always fascinated Her, and I see it here, following you like a haunted spirit. The thread of fate intertwines itself with you as it did with the three brothers. I believe *you* too are being tested."

Sorin was not sure what to make of that. It sounded like the ramblings of a tired old woman who had lived far longer than nature ever intended. But there was also something in her tone that said she knew more than she let on.

Before they could cross the threshold, she stopped them again. "Before you go, I would have a word with the Druid girl. Alone."

Sorin looked at Shaye, wrinkling his brow with worry. She nodded for him to go, and he obeyed, reluctantly; though concern for her clouded his thoughts.

CHAPTER SIXTEEN

Shaye

T*he door slammed* shut as Sorin left the dusty old cottage. Shaye hated it here; she had never liked cramped spaces. Atropani had been careless with her housekeeping, cobwebs occupied every corner and bowls were left dirty from spells she had used them for. Now the rancid stench of the Orc filled the small room, making it difficult to take a breath.

"I may not see your future, dear, but I see your past so very clearly." The chair across from Shaye creaked under the woman as she sat. She extended withered hands to her. Shaye hesitated, taking the seat across from her and giving her hands to the eerie old woman. The moment their hands touched, the fire went out, leaving the small cabin in pitch darkness. Shaye heard Atropani gasp, the sound of her own fast-paced breathing accompanying it.

Atropani hissed, "I sense much fear in you. Your past lingers in your dreams. Forgiveness will not come easily for you and the darkness that surrounds you will overtake you if you are not careful. I have seen it before." Grief was plain on her face.

"With the girl you spoke of."

"Yes. She tried desperately to fight the storm within her. For a while, it worked, and she was happy. But she made many mistakes along the way. Mistakes I hope you will be able to avoid. My advice to you, Shaye Wistari, is to not trust honeyed words from men. Should you allow yourself to be manipulated, should you give in to the anger in your heart, then yours will be a legacy of darkness."

Shaye tore her hands away from the Fate. "You said you couldn't see the future." She stood, stumbling, and grabbed a chair to steady herself. She was finding it difficult to navigate her way in the dark, unfamiliar cottage.

Atropani laughed, "I cannot see your future, but I can make predictions based on what I have seen in the past. Darkness has been around since the beginning, girl, and it shows itself often. History teaches us through the mistakes and triumphs of others." There was an edge to her voice now as, she added, "Heed my words, child, or all of Asterion will suffer for it."

A sudden gust of wind threw open the door and pushed Shaye out into the garden. She could hear the hag cackling behind her as the door shut. It was late evening by now, and the sun was hidden behind a cluster of trees, leaving a chill in the air.

The men looked exhausted and worried. Sorin especially, as he gripped a sword in his hand. All Shaye wanted was to put as much distance between her and this place as she could. She rushed past Sorin without a word and mounted Finn, ready to lead the way north. Sorin took her lead and called the men to do the same.

No one asked her about what had happened once Sorin had left her alone with Atropani. Sorin rode up next to her and Finn kicked his back leg out at Sorin's horse. Shaye patted him on the neck, "Easy Finn."

"He's right to be cross with me. I shouldn't have taken you in there."

"You did nothing wrong, Sorin. And I'm fine, I promise."

They rode quietly for a good while until Elijah filled the silence with a song. He sang of home, of fishing on the docks, and of basking in the sunshine. It distracted Shaye for a while, until he changed to a different, more familiar song. She was not sure where she had heard it before, but the tune came to her, buried deep within her memories.

She began to hum, thinking of the first flowers that would bloom in the palace gardens after a long, cold winter. They were still traveling along the barren road, the trees surrounding them as dead as if it were the end of fall and not the beginning of spring. Shaye began to sing as the words to the old Druid lullaby came to her. It was like a reflex, something that had lingered deep within her memories. She saw a woman with hair the color of autumn leaves, smiling down at her as she brushed Shaye's hair.

Elijah and the others went quiet as she sang. Moments later she realized they had stopped, allowing her to ride a few feet ahead of them. When she turned back, she was startled to see full blooms of flowers left in her wake. Leaves on the trees had come back to life, green and beautiful in the fullness of the small forest. She stopped singing then, and just as quickly as they had come, they were gone again.

Breathless, she started to laugh. She looked at Sorin, his eyes were alight in the wake of her magic. She had done the impossible, she had created life from her very own will. This time there was no headache. She had not even been trying to use her magic, it had come as naturally as breathing. The caw of a crow broke through her excitement, reminding her that she had more work to do. But for the first time, she thought maybe, *just maybe*, she was more capable than she had believed.

CHAPTER SEVENTEEN

Sorin

They were *nearly to the* lake that separated them from the Winter Palace before Sorin decided they would stop for the night. It had been weeks since the death of his father, and he felt as if they were not moving fast enough. But tension had been especially high today, and Shaye had spent the better part of the ride more reserved than before. They all needed to rest. The trip to see Atropani had shaken them all, and he had been full of concern for Shaye, until the moment on the road where her magic had brought the land back to life. It was as if a small seed of hope had been planted in her after that, and he did not want to push her too hard, afraid she would lose that seed.

His hope was that once she let her walls down, she would be able to tap into her magic more easily. They were only half a day's ride from the Winter Palace, and the closer they came, the worse the blight got. Fields turned brown and houses stood abandoned. Worst of all was the lingering sense of dread. He was not sure if that was from the blight itself or if he was just apprehensive about what was to come. Not to mention, he was not particularly looking forward to coming face to face with the other two Fates. If they looked anything like Atropani, he was without a doubt going to have nightmares.

At least he knew what they were to do now: find the Fates and ask them to take him to the place where his father had hidden Leto's Stave. From there they would decide what came next. He knew it was a shit plan, but the most urgent matter was to find the relic and make sure it was still intact. Best case scenario, with Shaye so close to the magic of the Raven Wood, her powers would awaken enough for her to easily call on them.

He hoped instinct would kick in like it had earlier and she would know what she needed to do to repair the relic. Worst case, they could take it back to the Summer Palace and find a Sorcerer with more experience. At least then, it would be surrounded by the palace guard and his army, safe from the darkness Atropani feared so much. Time was of the essence here, they just had to get to the Stave.

They were settling in, roasting a thin rabbit Elijah had trapped earlier. Even the wildlife was withering away, thanks to the blight, unable to get food and nourishment from the dying land. They would have to think of something if they were going to stay fed up here. To come all this way just to starve would be rather embarrassing.

Shaye was practicing incantations from an old spell book Sorin had brought. He knew she was trying her best; they were simple spells, the kind they used to teach to children. *This will work, it must.* He had to keep reminding himself of that. Now that a piece of her magic had been stirred up inside of her, she seemed much more optimistic while practicing. At the very least, she was not cursing as much while she worked.

"How about a break?" He smiled down at her.

"What do you have in mind?" She looked relieved when he offered her his hand.

"Just an evening stroll with the most beautiful creature here." He winked at her, as she put her arm through his.

"Ha, are you sure? Because Bron *is* awfully pretty."

"That oaf doesn't hold a candle to you, milady." They ventured away from the camp and down to a small, steady stream. It was beautiful in the evening light, he wondered if the blight had yet touched it. It was difficult to see his land, the country he loved with all his heart, being torn from the inside out.

Shaye looked thoughtful and he wondered if she was thinking the same things as him. He knew she was not ready to admit it, but they were alike in a lot of ways, and in another life, they could have been close friends.

"What do you say we take our minds off of things... Try to have some fun?"

She eyed him suspiciously. "What sort of *fun?*"

"The youthful sort." He began to unbutton his trousers.

"Sorin! I would advise you to put those back on immediately, before you catch more than a chill." She jokingly shoved him.

"It's an innocent swim, that's all." He removed his shirt and reveled in the cool breeze.

Shaye, to his surprise, took his lead, removing her boots. Moments later they stood, only in their undergarments, grinning ear to ear at one another. Shaye was the first to brave the water, Sorin following in a splash that took the breath from him. The water was much colder than he had expected.

They paddled further into the stream; it was shallow, as Sorin found when he dove down under the water. When he came back up for air, Shaye was close to him. He splashed at her, making her squeal.

Sorin floated onto his back, trying to appear casual. He

laughed at a bit of seaweed on her face. She touched her hair self-consciously, "What is it?"

He laughed again as she struggled to find whatever it was that was so amusing. "Sorin, what is so funny?"

He paddled over to her, pulling the seaweed from her cheek, and wiping away the mud it had left behind with his thumb. She allowed his hand to linger there. He was trying to ignore the urge to kiss her. He wanted to know what it would be like, just for a moment, to be normal with her. To be a man and a woman who could enjoy time together, who could come to love one another.

Instead, he pulled his hand away and asked, "So tell me, Shaye Wistari, is there some tall, dark, and handsome man waiting for you back home? Or on that ship of yours, perhaps?"

She scoffed at the insinuation, "Please. If you *smelled* the men on that ship then you wouldn't even be asking that question."

He was comforted by her answer, though he knew he had no right to be.

"And you? *King* Sorin, I'm sure you have courtiers lining up by the dozens back in the Summer Palace. Just awaiting your heroic return home, ready to lift their skirts at your call." She raised an eyebrow at him.

"If you talked to the girls at the Summer Palace, then *you* would not be asking *me* that question. A dull bunch, the lot of 'em." He watched for her reaction but saw none, to his disappointment. Sorin remained close to her. "As a matter of fact, I think the palace could use more women like you. Bold women who long for a better world, not a better dress."

"I never did like being at court. Not that I spent much time there, but I found it to be stuffy and the people to be pompous. Like everyone was constantly putting on some grand show. It always looked exhausting to me. I did everything I could to avoid being there. My friend and I would spend hours outside of the palace walls, going on epic quests that he had planned for us." She twirled a leaf that had fallen into the water, watching it spin around in the steady stream. Sorin couldn't take his eyes off her.

"Who would have guessed you'd really go on those great quests. First in the East, and now here." He floated on his back once more, looking up at the sky through the bare branches.

"Yes, who knew."

After they tired from their swim, they returned to shore, shivering as they put their clothes back on. The sky had grown darker, though there was enough light for them to find their way back to camp. Shaye was teasing him some more about his life at court when they approached the clearing.

He could sense that something was wrong as the hair on his arms stood on end. It was too quiet. He went on high alert, especially once he noticed the birds in the trees had gone silent. Years of hunting told him that silence like this signaled an approaching predator.

Before he could share his concern with the others, a hiss cut in from behind a tree up ahead. Elijah was standing guard, but did not see the creature until it was too late. He was slammed into a tree, crumpling to the ground with a troubling thud. The men barely had time to react before the monster was on them. Sorin and Anik unsheathed their swords, while Bron stepped in between Shaye and the horrifying creature. Sorin gave him a nod; no matter what, Bron was to keep Shaye safe.

Elijah still wasn't moving, and panic flooded Sorin's senses as he took in the terrifying snake-like creature standing before them. Black scales made up the long, serpentine body; but most horrifying was the human face it had: it was a *Naga*. The horses danced around, ready to bolt from where they were tied.

"Long way from home, King Sssorin." It taunted him with a voice that did not sound quite human. Sorin froze. "That'sss right, youngling, I know who you are. And I know what you have come for." The Naga sneered at him.

"Well in that case, if you wouldn't mind pointing us in the right direction, we'll be on our way." Sorin stepped to the side, drawing the creature away from Bron and Shaye. If he could get it to turn its back to them, then Bron would have an opening to run it through with his sword. The Orc had been full of brute strength; but if the books were correct, then the challenge here would be the Naga's speed.

"It iss not yoursss to take. You would usse it for your own gain. Humansss. You are all alike." The Naga snapped its venomous, inhuman teeth in warning. It was startling to see something so grotesque with such a human likeness.

"I don't want to fight you or any other creatures from the Raven Wood. But I *will* protect the people who cannot protect themselves. If I must fight you to do so, then I will." Sorin wielded his sword, ready to defend himself and the others.

The Naga sniffed the air, turning its snake-like eyes to Shaye. "Interessting. I haven't sseen your kind in more than a decade." Sorin felt fury surge through him as Shaye stiffened under the Naga's attention.

"She is of no concern to you." Sorin needed the beast to focus on him.

"She iss a traitor if she iss here helping *you*. There are ssome who would pay a fine sssum for her. Perhapss a trade iss in order. The Druid in exchange for what you sseek." The Naga was bobbing side to side, and Sorin feared the agility it likely possessed.

"Out of the question." Sorin was surprised by the Naga's offer. It occurred to him that the Naga's interest in her was perhaps a sign that they had been on the right track by bringing her with them. If she was powerful enough to warrant such a bounty, then she must be a threat to whatever darkness was causing the blight.

With the Naga's attention on Sorin again, Bron took his opening and lunged for the creature, just missing its scaled body as it slithered out of the way. They were going to have to be smart about this if they were going to make it out of here in one piece.

The Naga snapped around, as quick as a rattlesnake, tearing through Bron's gauntlet with its razor-sharp teeth. Blood began to seep through, and Sorin desperately tried to remember if the Naga's bite was venomous. He wished he had paid closer attention to the books he had read on them.

Bron let out a thunderous cry, swinging the massive sword toward the Naga. Sorin could not understand why it wasn't backing down. Naga were territorial, and right now it was nowhere near its nest in the Raven Wood. If it was protecting the relic, then they must be headed in the right direction; or, they were, at the very least, on the right track to finding it.

Before it could attack again, Sorin and Anik lunged. Just as Sorin swung his sword to make contact, the Naga was snatched up. Sorin stumbled as his sword hit the air. It screeched as it was pulled out of sight and into the trees. Sorin heard a loud crash in the distant forest, then silence followed as the men looked around, on guard for another attack.

Sorin looked around wildly for Shaye, finding that she was no longer where Bron had left her. She was beside Elijah, who was standing on unsteady feet untying the horses, and doing their best to calm them. Everyone was silent as they waited for the Naga to strike again.

Instead of a hiss from the snake-like monster, a giggle came from the tree. "Do you see the looks on their faces? I will admit that was quite enjoyable. Naga can be such bullies."

The men stepped back; Elijah was leaning on Shaye while Bron removed the gauntlet from his arm to inspect the damage. In front of them, a petite creature jumped down from the tree, barely making a sound as her small bare feet hit the dirt. She was like something from the ancient stories of Forest Dwellers that his grandmother had told him. Her skin was a soft shade of green, with eyes the color of moss and she stood no taller than Shaye's shoulder. Her hair was entangled with vines, making it difficult to distinguish where her hair ended and the vines began. Sorin had never seen anything, or anyone, like her. Then again, today seemed to be a day of firsts. He had never tangled with a Naga either.

"Who are you talking to?" He looked around for whoever she had been speaking to in the trees. She was a curious creature, staring at them with her head tilted to the side as if *they* were the magical Forest Dweller who had just appeared from the treetops.

"The trees, silly. They were happy to help you with your little pest problem. Naga talk a lot but they don't usually bother anyone unless provoked." The small girl paused and gave a little frown, "Did you?"

"Provoke it? No, we... we're just here to get something that belonged to my father." Sorin thought she looked relatively harmless, but after the week he'd had, he did not want to take any chances.

"We know all about that, don't we?" Again, she was speaking as if someone was standing beside her. Sorin noticed that a swarm of moths were fluttering around her. He wondered if she was talking to them or to herself.

It was getting darker, and they were wasting time they could not afford. He felt a sense of urgency now that word had spread about their presence, and he worried that they would have more company soon. With two of his men injured, he needed to find them cover, and fast.

"We appreciate your... and the tree's, help, but we really have to be going." He grabbed Shaye by the elbow and backed them away from the Forest Dweller slowly. He realized with a start that it was true the Raven Wood's magical creatures were venturing away from their homes and heading further south. The fact that she or the Naga had been able to cross the threshold at the forest's edge confirmed what they had suspected. The Stave was no longer working. This was bad.

"But your friend is hurt. I can help with that. I am quite gifted with healing. I am well known for it within my clan. May I?" Before any of them could answer her, she steered Bron to a nearby tree stump. He looked at her in protest, but she was insistent.

Shaye leaned into Sorin; she and Elijah had untied the horses and she handed him a set of reins. "Maybe we should give her a chance. He can't travel like this. Especially if more creatures come. We need him ready to fight." Shaye was surprisingly calm and collected after what had just happened.

"You're right." He turned to the dweller, who was poking and prodding at Bron's armor in fascination. To her he said, "You can help; but could I ask one more thing of you...?"

"Mavka! I am Mavka of the highland clan." Something made her giggle as she pulled a muddy-looking salve out of the pack slung around her back. Sorin vaguely remembered the books he had read on the Raven Wood's clans. They were made up of seven groups of Forest Dwellers. The Dwellers were an ancient people who kept to the trees. They relied heavily on nature and secrecy, secluding themselves from the rest of society.

Mavka held Bron's strong arm in her dainty hands. "It's a good thing I'm here; those Naga bites can lead to nasty infections." She got to work on him, applying the stinking paste to his wound and wrapping it in leaves. Bron wrinkled his nose in disgust, but did as she directed him.

Sorin continued, trying to capture her attention again,

"Mavka, how do the creatures know about us and why we're here?"

"The trees have been talking." She giggled again, and the moths danced wildly around her. "They say you've come to set things right. They say it is a debt you owe to the land. My father has been frantically awaiting your arrival." She finished with Bron, releasing him. Then she stood, and twirled around, dancing to the rhythm of the moths around her. She motioned for Elijah to sit next, eyeing him for visible injuries from the hit he took.

"Mavka..." Sorin cleared his throat, stepping carefully towards her like she was a doe in the wood that would be spooked off at any moment. "Do you know where the relic is?"

She stopped, suddenly growing serious. The giggling ceased and the moths around her seemed to retreat to the shadows. "First you must answer us, young King. Are you here to settle your debts?" She was smiling, but there was a venom behind those words.

"I am here to stop this blight that is affecting the crops. It is my duty to the people of Asterion."

Anger flashed across Mavka's delicate, pointed face. He had said the wrong thing.

"And what of us? The magical creatures here in the North that your father has kept isolated and alone. To be subjected to Nefari rule."

Nefari? That word was familiar to Sorin. He knew it from the history books. The Nefari were an ancient group of rogue Magi who had been so hungry for power that they had tapped into dark magic. Sacrifices and bloodlettings were their power source. But they had been gone for almost a decade... Sorin had not even considered the possibility of rogue Magi being responsible for what was happening in the North. Things had been quiet for so long; his father had gotten too comfortable. It had been careless of him to not keep patrols on the border.

The Nefari could be the reason the Stave was not working anymore. They could be the darkness that Atropani warned them about. That would also explain the blight and the fog on the sea; something like these required powerful magic and malice. If he was right, then they did not stand a chance. Even with Shaye tapping into her powers, there was no way she would be able to defend them against an organized and experienced group of dark Magi.

Mavka flinched, her eyes were suddenly wild with fear. In a hushed tone she said, "Run."

Sorin felt it before he saw it; it was like living *dread*. Looking behind them, he saw a dark fog creeping across the foliage, slow but sure in its intent. It was headed for the clearing where they stood defenseless. The horses had sensed it first; Finn nudged Shaye, nearly knocking her off her feet. Sorin steadied her and watched as the horses took off without them. They ran in the direction that Mavka had gone. Finn reared up, pulling from Shaye's grasp to join the other horses. On instinct, Sorin grabbed onto Shaye's hand. Her fingers gripped him, familiar under his own calloused ones. And they ran.

They followed Mavka through the tree lines, and Sorin realized they were on the outskirts of Lake Brenmar. He caught glimpses of the sparkling water through the trees. Shaye was panting behind him, and every so often she would stumble. He held tight to her, refusing to let the fog catch up to them. Bron and Anik were to the right of him, but Elijah was struggling to keep up. His wounds from the Naga must have been worse than they had thought. Sorin cursed the horses for bolting.

Bron must have realized it at the same time; he fell back, intent on reaching Elijah before the fog. Elijah fell, a sickening crunch coming from his ankle. Before Bron could reach him, the black mist engulfed him completely. Almost as if devouring him. There was a scream and then silence. Elijah was gone.

"Bron, we can't outrun it! We need cover." As desperately as he wanted to go back for his friend, they had to keep pushing forward if they wanted to stay alive.

Mavka yelled from ahead, "There is only one place that can offer that! It's just ahead!" He could have sworn she was slowing her pace so they would not lose sight of her and where she was going. He was grateful for it. The moon's light was shining bright, but it was still difficult to navigate the uneven ground beneath their feet.

Sorin saw the cover she meant. The Winter Palace. He hadn't realized they had been so close to it, but there it was. Its grand, white, stone walls loomed over the lake, shining like a beacon for them in the night.

"It's too far!" Shaye shouted from beside him. Her face was flushed, and he was surprised to see more anger than fear there. Before he could respond, she pulled her hand away from his. He scrambled to grab her, but it was too late.

Shaye faced the fog. It moved as if it were a living creature, and Sorin saw it hesitate at her presence. In fact, it coiled away from her. A hideous scream sounded from inside of it, an inhuman sound that would haunt his dreams for years to come.

The way the fog stopped before her, it was as if it was willing to obey her. His mind had to be playing tricks, but he swore it was acting as if it recognized her.

Shaye stood firmly in place. "I am done running. Do you hear me? I am *done*." The ground beneath their feet shuddered in response to her proclamation. The earth heeded her call, trembling in defiance of the fog that was not welcome there. Then, as quickly as it had appeared, the black fog vanished, leaving no trace of its existence. Only the sound of Sorin's heartbeat thudding in his ears remained, along with the darkness of night.

Shaye turned toward them; tears were streaming down her face, but the defiant look in her eyes still lingered. He was not sure how, but she had just reclaimed her power.

CHAPTER EIGHTEEN

Shaye

Shaye *was still trembling* when they reached the palace doors. The run had been embarrassingly tiring, but using her powers after having had them lie dormant for so long had taken an even bigger toll. She tried not to show the exhaustion that she was feeling. How was she to restore one of the most powerful magical objects in their world if she could barely even conjure enough strength to fend off the black fog? Okay, *man-eating* fog. But even so, she was in way over her head.

She was relieved to see that the horses had reached the palace safely. They lingered nearby, nibbling on patches of grass. Finn wandered to her with his head bowed low. Shaye patted the sorry beast, "It's okay, I was scared too."

Anik grabbed the horses' reins and led them to the stables Shaye had told him were around back. His eyes were filled with tears, and he seemed eager to be alone, to grieve the loss of their friend in private.

She could feel Sorin watching her. She had noticed a lot of that lately, and was surprised to find that she didn't mind it. She gave him a small smile, hoping he wouldn't notice how her hands still shook at her sides. She stuffed them into her pockets and looked around. One of the others had lit candles in the grand entryway of the palace.

Shaye took a moment to soak in the state of her childhood home. She had only lived in the palace for a few short years, but it had been a safe haven for her after the loss of her parents. She had little to no memory of her home before the palace and her parents' deaths, so this was all she had known. It was where she had gone to school, where she had celebrated holidays and birthdays, where she had made her first true friend.

It was eerie how little had changed after all these years. Almost like the palace was preserved, frozen in time. Cobwebs hung in the corners and dust settled on the banisters of the grand staircase, but it was as if the stone-clad building was waiting patiently for its residents to return from a long trip. It was not until she saw the ballroom entrance, where a tray of shattered glass lay within sight, that her heart broke again at the memory of the Winter Solstice. The carpet was stained a dark purple, from blood or wine, she was not sure.

She had heard rumors once she was older that King Allerick had ordered the palace to be cleaned after the coup. Bodies had been given final resting rites, but it seemed his men were only thorough with the bodies, not the rest of the mess they had left behind. She almost laughed out loud at the bitter thoughts racing through her mind. *Seems they were not thorough enough in more ways than one.* King Allerick had singlehandedly stripped the Magi of their magic, just as the old king had stripped the common man of their comforts. And in the process King Allerick had unknowingly set his son up to face the dark consequences of his actions.

She hated when these dark thoughts crept into her mind. The rage that accompanied them was sometimes too much for her. It is why she had quit the Guild. She found herself resenting the men she was working with on the Asterion ships; and when she had gone to Sagon, she had found her escape. A place where no one cared that she was a Magi. Captain Thorsten and his group of vagabonds had understood; they were all running from something. They had never asked questions, never judged. She had been free.

What am I doing here? She ran a hand through her tangled hair. Again, distant memories of someone pulling her away from that very ballroom lingered in her mind. A boy with large blue eyes holding a finger to his lips. And then darkness. The next thing she remembered was coming out of that tree line and stumbling right into her new life.

Sorin was at her side, though she had not heard him approach. He grabbed her elbow, pulling her in close, and spoke gently in her ear. "If this is too much, we can find another place to stay for the night. You don't have to do this."

The kindness in his voice made her hold back a sob. He had just lost a man who had been a brother to him, yet he was still taking the time to worry about her. This was the last place in the world she wanted to be. But after losing Elijah to the fog, it was hard to tell what other creatures were going bump in the night out there. Ironically, this was the safest place for them. She shook her head and took a steadying breath.

"Thank you, but I'm fine."

Anik rejoined them and she pulled away from Sorin, walking toward the large staircase leading to two separate wings. Shaye didn't miss the knowing look Anik gave Sorin, but she ignored it. "I can show you all to the rooms. We can try to get the fireplaces going, maybe even find fresh clothes." They were all sweat-stained and tired. The screams of Elijah echoed in her mind. She felt dizzy, but she wasn't sure if it was from the adrenaline or the horror of the last few days finally catching up to her.

The group quietly followed her. The exhaustion of the day

showed in every step they took. Grief weighed heavily on them. Shaye had not known Elijah well, but he had been kind to her. He had been well mannered and respectful, and had sung beautifully. She had gathered from the way the men had interacted that they had all been close. They had often told stories on the road of growing up together. Suddenly there was a large pit in her stomach, guilt hitting her like a punch to the gut.

I should have saved him. I should have been practicing my magic more on the road, then I could have stopped it sooner. They arrived in a hallway lined with solid, blue-painted doors. The white trim around them was lined with little blue flowers. Shaye touched the delicate details in wonder. She had loved these flowers, loved all the details carefully placed throughout the palace. When she first arrived at the palace as a child, she had spent her first few days exploring the endless halls and rooms.

She could remember thinking that she had never seen anything so glorious in all her young life. Her favorite were the ornate birds that filled the walls inside of the rooms in the east wing. These rooms were where Idor's guests had stayed; she could not bring herself to take her companions to the west wing where she had once laid her head as a girl. Where she had lived with her aunt and uncle and the other aristocrats of court.

She used to sneak into this wing with Bastian to spy on the noble men and women visiting the court. Nanny Jin had explicitly warned them to stay out of sight, but that made the adventure all the more exciting. Shaye shivered at the memories. It pained her to think of Bastian, especially here in the place they had called home. She wondered if Sorin could help her search for any record of him in King Allerick's registration when this was over. Though, as much as she hated to admit it, he had likely perished with the others on that horrible night.

"Here we are." She waited in the hall filled with unoccupied rooms; they had not discussed sleeping arrangements yet. Up until now, Sorin had been able to keep an eye on her from across a campfire. They had gotten used to being near each other and it seemed that now the others were also unsure of what to do next.

Sorin spoke first, "Before everyone heads off to their respective rooms to count sheep, I think we're forgetting about something." He raised a brow and tilted his head at the pixie-girl who was currently examining Bron's jacket, hands tugging on the buttons in strange interest. Bron stood straight, ever the good soldier, doing his best to ignore the strange female at his side.

Shaye let out a snort. She covered her mouth, just as shocked at herself as everyone around her seemed to be. Sorin laughed next and soon they were all laughing. Everyone except Bron who clearly did not see the amusement at his expense. Even Mavka giggled, although Shaye wasn't sure the girl really knew why they had been laughing.

Sorin regarded the Forest Dweller, "You have done us a great service. We owe you our lives. If there is anything we can do for you..."

"I would very much like to stay," Mavka interrupted hopefully, looking at all of them with her strange, murky eyes. "You will need a guide, and no one knows the forest as I do."

Shaye did not doubt that. Mavka was born of the Raven Wood, from an ancient line of magical creatures who had not been seen by many in hundreds of years. Her people kept to the safety of the canopy. If anyone could be their guide through the dangers of the forest and to the Fates or whatever else awaited them, it would be her. For all the trouble they had gone through with the Orc, Atropani had not been able to give them much more than a riddle that needed solving. *Follow the Northern Stars.* Looking at the strange Forest

Dweller that had found them as soon as they had reached the North, Shaye thought that maybe that is what Atropani had expected to happen.

Sorin must have agreed. "Mavka, it would be an honor." He swept an extravagant bow toward her. Shaye was surprised at how easily he welcomed her into their fold; after all, his father had feared creatures like Mavka, banishing them to the North. For him to put faith in not one, but two girls with magical abilities told her that maybe she was right about him being different from his father.

CHAPTER NINETEEN

Shaye

O*nce everyone parted* ways to their own private rooms, Shaye found herself laying in a luxurious bed, staring at the elaborate four posts that made it up. It had been so long since she had laid in a bed like this; she relished the soft, feather down pillows and warm comforting blankets wrapped around her. Despite the comfort she found herself in, she was having trouble sleeping.

The shadows were closing in around her again. She feared the ghosts that would surely visit her in her nightmares; so instead, she went in search of Sorin. She wasn't sure why, but she sensed that maybe he was haunted by ghosts of the past like she was. It surprised her how much she was missing his presence, having been with him constantly these past weeks.

It took a bit of searching the abandoned halls, but eventually she found him in the library. The room was quiet, and she spotted Sorin at a desk near the window, the moonlight shining on him. Three empty glasses sat beside him; Shaye guessed that Bron and Anik had joined him in a farewell drink to the friend they had just lost. She was glad she had not come earlier; she had no right to interrupt something like that.

He looked up with a troubled expression when he noticed her there. "Shaye, is everything okay?"

"Just some trouble sleeping. You?" She ventured closer, into the dusty room still filled with rare and expensive books. Some part of her was grateful that King Allerick's men had not looted the Winter Palace. She was not sure if it was meant as a gesture of respect, but nonetheless it made some piece of her feel thankful.

"More research." He gestured to the books strewn around the table. Some were ancient looking, pages worn at the edges, and some were written in languages she had never seen. "The King Idor was quite the collector. It is a shame my father left these books abandoned for so long. He was never the scholarly type; he preferred getting his hands dirty." He ran a tanned hand along the book in front of him. His hair was falling slightly into his eyes. He had not cut it since they had been in Aramoor. She had a slight urge to brush it from his face, wondering how it would feel under her fingers.

Shaye looked down at the mention of his father; it was a hard topic for her. She changed the subject. "It was kind of you to allow Mavka to stay." She laughed. "She seems quite taken with Bron."

Sorin laughed with her, "Bron is a big softy deep down. I'm not a gambling man, unlike yourself," he gave her a sly dimpled smirk, "but judging by how hard he tries to ignore her, I would wager he's taken with her as well."

"Ha, he has a funny way of showing it." Shaye rearranged some books sitting on a table near her, keeping her hands busy to mask how nervous she suddenly was to be alone in a room with Sorin. She realized this was the first time the two of them had been alone since their swim in the stream.

"Bron had a tough upbringing. His father is a warrior

through and through. He wanted Bron and the rest of us to be the same way. Although his father meant well, Bron didn't grow up learning what tenderness was." He moved from the desk and came to where she stood in the center of the massive room. He had changed into a simple linen shirt and dark trousers. "Not all of us can live life as boldly as you."

Shaye tucked her hair behind her ear. "Some would call me foolish."

"Not me." He reached for her, but she pulled away slightly out of instinct. They had grown close over the course of their journey, but now that they were in the Winter Palace, she felt guilty. She was afraid of letting him in, of feeling like a traitor to her people. She might have come on this quest so she could help the people of Asterion, but she would not forgive the treatment of the Magi or the slaughter she had witnessed as a child. Or the poor treatment she still witnessed in the harbour.

Atropani's words rang in her mind, *a legacy of darkness.* What would *her* legacy be?

"Can I ask you something?" This time Shaye decided to be as bold as he believed her to be. "How can you believe in me and trust someone like Mavka? Do you not support your father's beliefs that magic is a danger to the people of Asterion?"

Sorin was quiet, thoughtful, before he answered her. "Shaye, I believe in equality. Not just for mortals but for Magi as well. If *we* can work together, you, me, and Mavka... building relations between humans and Magi, then how can anyone tell us that the same isn't possible with all of Asterion?"

This time Shaye did not move away when he closed the gap between them. He smelled of citrus and sandalwood, and she was suddenly very self-conscious of her unbrushed hair and the thin nightgown she was wearing, covered only by a silk robe.

"Now can I ask *you* something?" He pushed the hair from her face, his fingers lingering there for a moment before smiling broadly. "Dance with me?"

"There's no music." She cocked her head to the side in amusement.

"Humor a naive king, please. After the week we have had, I just want to be here, with you." Sorin stepped back, extending a hand to her. She took it. *Be bold,* she told herself.

They danced, moving gracefully in the moonlit room. He spun her and they both laughed. Shaye wanted so desperately to believe him. To believe that she could convince him to change things once this was all over. His words had been filled with such hope and passion and, in that moment, when he pulled her into him signaling the end of their dance, she decided to trust him.

They were so close that she could feel his heart beating. His eyes were dark blue pools, intense with something she had not noticed before. "Shaye, I..." Before he could finish, she stood on her tippy toes to kiss him. At first, he did not move, stunned by the action. Then she felt him give himself to her, pulling her closer, hungry for more. He tasted of strawberry wine, reminding her of a warm summer night.

Shaye pulled back a little, surprised at herself. It was not like she had not been with a man before, but this felt different. This kiss felt both tender and powerful, like a shift in the universe itself. She wanted more, but the reality of where they were and who he was set in again. "I'm sorry, Your Majesty." She backed up, bowing her head. "That was out of line."

Before he could say anything, she hurried from the room. Once back in the privacy of her chambers, she took a deep, steadying breath. Leaning against the big wooden door she brushed the hair from her face and thought to herself, *too bold.*

CHAPTER TWENTY

Sorin

In the morning, Sorin woke with a blistering headache. It had been a long night and he had drunk more than he should have. He, Bron, and Anik had spent the better part of the night drinking from an old bottle of mulled wine, first reminiscing about boyhood stories of Elijah, and then coming up with a plan. They would honor Elijah properly when this was all over.

The Naga and the man-eating fog had confirmed, yet again, what they had suspected. The Stave had been rendered ineffective. The next matter at hand was: would they be able to salvage it, or had someone taken it? The mention of Nefari had shaken them. Even Bron and Anik had heard the stories as children. The Nefari haunted the tales mothers and nursery maids told naughty boys to scare them into behaving. Even the strongest Sorcerers had feared them.

If what Mavka said was true, then the Nefari would be prepared for them. They would have had years to organize any sort of trouble they planned to make. It seemed likely to Sorin that they had been biding their time until they found a moment of weakness. If that was the case, then it made sense that the blight had only begun when his father had gotten sick. The men all agreed that they needed to get to the Stave as quickly and as quietly as possible.

Bron and Anik had agreed to leave at first light to scout the areas around the palace grounds and near the Raven Wood. Bron woke Mavka before heading to bed, to discuss the plan with her, and she had generously agreed to be their guide to track down Atropani's sisters, Clothsari and Lachtori. The forest girl was strange, but he had to admit that there was something endearing about her that made it easy to trust her.

Shaye was another puzzle to solve. Sorin had no idea where her head was at after what had happened last night. He had spent all morning trying to wrap his head around their moment in the library. It felt like a dream, being there with her in the dim light, the taste of her on his lips. He was not sure if the kiss had been about the guilt she had been feeling about Elijah, or if it was something more. The kiss had caught them both off guard, but he had welcomed it. He'd been glad she had done it. Until she ran away, that is. It seemed like every time she started to let herself trust him, she would retreat twice as far back away from him.

That was why he was searching for her now. Unsure of when they would be returning, he had decided to forgo his armor; traveling light would save them the time and energy they desperately needed. His sword was strapped to his back, and he placed multiple daggers on his person. More than anything, he wanted to make sure they did not lose anyone else on this journey.

Shaye's room was empty, the bed clearly slept in. So he decided to venture downstairs. He ran his hand along the mahogany banister, hand-carved with vines and flowers. It was incredible craftsmanship and he wondered if it had been made by human or Magi. The difference between the Summer and Winter Palaces was striking. The Summer Palace was well designed and practical, it paled in comparison to the grandeur of the Winter Palace.

In contrast, here, ornate carvings could be found around every corner, lavish artwork lined the walls, and open crystal chandeliers were in practically every room. King Idor had certainly spared no expense when it came to the luxurious home of his court. It was no wonder he had rarely left to venture south. And why he had never seen the rebellion coming.

King Idor had not taken the time to know his subjects, to listen to them and the unrest they were feeling. Sorin had often wondered if he had even known of the poor treatment his Sorcerers and nobles had subjected the people to. Or had he been too busy living in his perfect little world, isolated in blissful ignorance?

He descended the long staircase, spotting Shaye by the ballroom door. He could see from her profile that she had a thoughtful expression on her sun-kissed face. This could not be easy for her.

"We could close the door, you know?" He was kicking himself for not doing it earlier. He had meant to close the ballroom door before she awoke, to shield her from the bad memories and the feelings that must accompany them.

Turning to him, she sighed, "I was just thinking about how worried I'd been before the ball, about the trouble I'd be in for getting dirt on my new dress. It all seems so silly and insignificant now." She looked back to the ballroom. He noted the mess of it; broken glass and overturned tables littered the once glorious room. A few of the imported rugs had been removed with the bodies, but he could spot a dark stain here and there on the rugs that remained.

"You were just a kid. There's nothing you could have done." He knew what was really bothering her. It was regret at not being powerful enough to save them. He knew, because he felt it too.

"And yesterday?" Her jaw twitched. "I could have saved him, Elijah, if I had drawn my power sooner. I could have saved your friend. Just like the night of the spring festival and the Solstice. I failed my family, my best friend, and now I have failed Elijah... and you." She looked up at Sorin, searching his face. "I'm truly sorry."

He grabbed her hands and felt her tense up, but he did not let go. He needed her to know that he was sincere. They moved closer and he could feel the heat of her body near his own. He needed to tell her everything, to trust her. If they were going to get through this, then they *needed* to trust each other, to be able to rely on one another. "Shaye. That night, in the ballroom, I..."

"Sire. We're ready when you are." Anik stood at the entrance. Sweat glistened on his face. They must have gone all the way to the Raven Wood's border while patrolling the palace grounds.

Shaye was still looking at him, waiting for him to finish. He had wanted to tell her that there was nothing to forgive. That he understood, had felt that same sense of failure, because he had not been able to save them *all* that night. Because he had chosen to save *her* instead; but it would have to wait. Right now he needed to put his duty as king ahead of his feelings.

"It can wait." He offered a hand to Shaye and she took it. They walked through the door and out into the sunlight, leaving the palace behind, in search of the Fates.

CHAPTER TWENTY-ONE

Shaye

S *haye was annoyed* and distracted as they trudged through the Raven Wood. Finn walked obediently, dodging fallen branches. She patted his neck, letting him know she appreciated his efforts. Still, she could barely focus on the task at hand. She was too busy thinking about the way Sorin's hand had gripped hers near the ballroom door. She thought of how close his body had been to hers. He had been nervous, ready to tell her something, and she desperately wanted to continue the conversation.

She could not believe that she was behaving this way. Allowing herself to feel something, even for a second, for the son of her enemy. She was here on this journey for Brina and for her friends waiting to find a way back through the sea to Sagon. That was it, she told herself. There was no room for anything else, especially not a charming king with a dimple on her cheek.

Focus. She shook her head and looked up. They had been walking for a while now and she noticed that the further into the forest they got, the stranger things became. The canopy above them was scarce. What was once a vibrant and magical place was now... *dying.*

Her stomach turned and she wished she had not eaten so much at breakfast. She caught sight of a sickly rabbit in one of the scarce-looking brushes. It broke her heart as she recalled the fat rabbits that used to roam these woods, and how she had spent hours trying to set box traps for them as a child, just so she could pet their soft fur.

She had adored this forest back then, spending many days with Bastian, hiding from Nanny Jin, the no-nonsense woman in charge of them, and their Magi instructors. It had been a sanctuary to them with its ancient, towering trees to protect them from the scorn of every adult in their life. The brush was once thick and wild with life. Fascinating creatures had resided here, from friendly Pixies to fierce Fenrir, all equally free to live the way nature intended.

The desolate forest that she was looking at now was not at all what she had remembered. "This isn't right." Nausea was building in her and sweat beaded her temples.

Mavka was whispering to herself again, at least; that was what it looked like. Shaye had suspected for some time that she was talking to the moths that swarmed her like little shadows, though she still had not asked.

Mavka spoke to Shaye now. "For a while everything was as it had always been. We did not feel the effect of the new king's regime. Magic still radiated from the land here and we continued living in harmony, as we have since The Mother first created life. But then the Nefari came, like demons in the night. They have been here ever since, rotting the earth with their darkness." Disgust adorned her beautiful face as she spoke.

Shaye shivered. "That's why creatures like you and the Naga are heading south. Because the forest is rotting away, thanks to the Nefari presence." Sorin had caught her up on what he had discussed with the others the night before - That what they were facing could be the work of this ancient organization.

Anik snorted, "Nefari are monsters made up to scare children into behaving."

Shaye shook her head at him, brow furrowed. Nefari were dark magic users. They practiced blood and sacrificial magic, which had always been forbidden amongst her people. Black magic users were shunned and exiled to The Beyond. Nobody knew what happened to them after that as no one had ever returned from the other side of those mountains.

She recalled seeing a dark Magi as a child: a man who had been brought before her uncle and the Magi council to plead his case. He was accused of trying to bring his wife back from the dead. In the process, the man had lost his sight, a price for practicing the unnatural magic.

He had been convincing of his innocence, claiming he had no idea the spell given to him was a dark enchantment. The council had been ready to release him with a warning until the guards removed the wool gloves from his hands. They were ink black all the way to his wrists. Black hands were the tell-tale sign of a Nefari, and it was then that he was sentenced.

Even her uncle had recoiled at the horrid sight. It was like the black magic had infected him, spreading through his body, and devouring any human part of him until there was nothing left.

Strong magic always left a mark. That was why her teachers had always been quick to lose their patience with her as a child. They had believed her inhuman golden eyes were a sign of her strength, and when she failed to perform incantations and spells to their liking, they had accused her of being lazy and stubborn.

She had seen firsthand that black magic left a different

kind of mark, a mark of something much more sinister. "They're as real as we are Anik. Trust me."

A crow echoed above them, making Mavka smile.

"Friend of yours?" Shaye asked.

"Friend of *yours* actually. He says *welcome home*."

They traveled for the better part of the day before Mavka stopped in a clearing.

"This is where we wait."

"For what?" Sorin looked as exhausted as Shaye felt.

"For the North Star. It will guide us to the Fates' dwelling. Their magic guards its location, keeping them hidden from anyone wishing to find them and use them for their gifts."

"Keeping them hidden from us, you mean?" It was just as Atropani had said.

Mavka sat in a bed of brown leaves. "Exactly. So, we rest until nightfall, then we follow the star." She laid down where she sat. "Bron can sleep next to me."

Bron looked to Sorin for help, but he had no intention of providing any. Sorin was laughing as he began setting up camp. Bron and Mavka laid within arm's length of one another and Shaye and Sorin settled in nearby on the other side of the fire, while Anik laid up against a log.

It was nearing dusk; they had eaten a small meal and shared stories around the fire. Shaye even decided to share some tales from her time at sea with the great Captain Thorsten and his crew. She left out the incriminating bits, but everyone seemed to be fascinated by what she had to say. She was coming to the end of a particularly interesting tale of how she and her friends had talked their way out of a Padsu jail by calling in a favor from the King of Sagon, who it had turned out owed her captain a favor. All eyes were locked on her as she finished.

Sorin was smiling at her; shifting uncomfortably, she tucked a piece of hair behind her ear as she asked, "What?"

"Nothing. It's just... You have a glow about you when you talk about your adventures."

Shaye blushed, all eyes still on her, "It was the only time I've ever felt free. Like the burden of my past couldn't follow me as long as I kept moving."

Mavka chimed in, "I've always dreamed of daring adventures. Finding you is the closest I have ever come to leaving the Raven Wood. It is all I have ever known, and, believe me, I have explored everything I possibly can in here. It's my home, but I know there's so much more out there." She gazed sadly into the fire. Bron nudged her playfully in the shoulder, bringing a small smile to her lips.

It was quiet for a while, until Bron broke the silence with a story about the time he and Sorin had stolen a weapons cache from a group of mountain men in Skag. They all laughed at the tale, passing a small flask around the circle and forgetting for just a moment what waited for them when the stars came out.

A while later, they decided to try to get some sleep before heading out. Shaye stared up at the night sky waiting for the Northern Lights to appear, but they never did. She turned on her bedroll to whisper across the fire, "Mavka, where are the lights?"

Mavka sighed sadly, "Gone since the blight began. They were the first to fade away."

Shaye fell asleep thinking of the deep sadness in Mavka's voice, and it was no sooner that the nightmares began again. She was in the stairwell this time, a hand gripping her arm. It held onto her so tightly that she felt a bruise begin to form.

It pulled her out of a servant's entrance and into the forest. She could only see the shadow of a boy urging her to run. Above her, a murder of crows flew in the direction she was heading. Behind her she could hear cries for help and, when she looked, the dense, black fog was closing in on her.

She stopped when she and the shadow boy came to a cliff. *Jump*, his faint whisper urged her. She shook her head, tears streaming down her face. *Jump, for you will not fall. You will fly.* The crows circled around her now. She could not tell if the whisper was coming from them or from the boy she still could not make out.

When she did not listen, the hand pulled her hard toward the edge. *Jump and you will be free.* Shaye took a step closer to the edge; looking down, she could only see white light. It was warm and welcoming, a better option than what awaited her should she turn around or stay on the cliff. She closed her eyes tight and took another step.

Before she could plunge below, someone yanked her back. She struggled, trying to go into the warm white light. Whoever had pulled her away from the ledge was shaking her now. "Wake up, Shaye. Dammit wake up!"

She opened her eyes to find that Sorin was holding her tight to his chest. The realization of what had just happened took her breath away. She had been sleepwalking. She pulled away from him gently and looked around, still clutching him. She was standing on a cliff like the one in her dream. Only peace and warmth did not await her below. Instead, the thick black fog that had taken Elijah rumbled in its place. Her arm throbbed where the hand had held her and, when she looked down, a purplish-blue bruise was there in the shape of a man's hand.

Shaye began to cry when she realized what she had been about to do. Sorin held her, resting his head on hers. He kissed her hair as she let all the fear and anguish out. She could still hear the faint whisper of the fog calling to her from below. She clung to Sorin tighter, still shaking and out of breath. He murmured something into her hair that she could not quite make out. His arms were warm around her, holding tight as if he were afraid that she would vanish if he released her for even a second.

They stayed like that until Mavka appeared. Shaye looked at her friend from beneath Sorin's embrace, not ready to let go yet. Mavka looked at her apologetically, worry clouding her eyes. Shaye could tell Mavka did not want to interrupt, but they both knew this could not wait.

"It is time." She pointed a green finger to the sky where the North Star shined brightly, beckoning them onward.

CHAPTER TWENTY-TWO

Sorin

A*tropani had been right,* the star had led them straight
to her sisters. This cabin differed from the one Atropani
dwelled in. It was strange looking to say the least, built of
mossy wood and standing two stories high. It sat at a crooked
angle, and Sorin feared it might topple at any moment.

"What a shithole," Bron grumbled beside him. Next to him,
Mavka stood as close as she could; she repeated his words like
they were the first time she had heard such language, and
giggled to herself. Sorin laughed to himself. It was endearing
how much she wanted to learn about the mortal world.

He looked at the house in front of them. *And what is it that
we will learn here?* He led the way to the front door, noticing
with a start that it was already a jar. The doorknob was
broken, and he noticed bloody fingerprints on the dark wood.

He drew his sword, pushing the door open gently. He
signaled to Bron and Anik, who took his lead and held their
swords out in front of them. Something was wrong here, and
he worried they may be walking into an ambush.

"Stay out here," he ordered Shaye and Mavka, although he had a feeling they would not listen.

Inside, furniture was scattered throughout the room. A fire still raged underneath a large cauldron; whatever had happened here had happened recently. The men spread out to search for the sisters. Bron took the upstairs, the rickety staircase creaking under his weight. Anik went around back to check the perimeter. Sorin was having trouble seeing in the dark room. Broken glass crunched beneath his feet, signs of foul play.

Mavka shouted for Sorin. Behind an overturned sofa lay a woman who resembled Atropani. In contrast to her sister's white-gray hair, hers was dark, streaked with white. He was not sure which sister this was, but he had a sick feeling in his gut that it was the one they needed to speak to. Her throat had been cut, and the smell of sulfur radiated from the wound... No doubt the work of dark magic. To kill such a powerful being would take more power than any common Magi could muster. It was clear that someone had not wanted her to talk.

Shaye gasped and pulled on Sorin's sleeve. A few feet away, in the dark corner, sat the third sister. Tears of blood streamed from her hollowed eyes. Where her mouth should have been was now a cloud of dark fog, like the one from the forest. It shifted and moved as she struggled to speak, but the fog would not submit.

Shaye crawled to her, tears streaming down her own beautiful face now. "I need to help her." Sorin watched quietly as she tried to summon her magic in vain. Mavka touched her softly on the shoulder.

"There's nothing you can do. This sort of black magic cannot be broken so easily. It would likely require the death of the one who wielded it." Mavka was pulling a powder from her pack. "This should ease her pain."

"What sort of dark magic is this, Mavka? Even the Nefari

cannot possibly be powerful enough to destroy an immortal." Sorin thought back to the history books and could not recall any information on magic this strong.

Mavka shook her head sadly. "You are right, King Sorin. There is no magic in our realm that is powerful enough to do this sort of damage. I fear that the Nefari have found an ally from the Shadow Lands."

"Shadow Lands?"

Shaye answered for Mavka, "The Beyond, Sorin. They have found help from The Beyond."

"That doesn't make any sense. Could they really be strong enough for such a thing?"

"They could if they wielded a relic of their own. If they had the Obsidian pendant of Pris, then they would have the ability to control the shadows." Mavka held the Fate's hand in her own, trying to offer the woman comfort. "Long ago, after Pris and his act of vengeance, the Obsidian fell to an ancient clan. The family who controlled it were thought to be cursed. They were called *Shadow Dancers*. My father and the other clan leaders thought the relic to be lost. It seems they were wrong." She let the Fate's hand slip down to her tattered gown and wiped the bloody tears from the helpless woman's face.

The Fate reached out her hand, beckoning him toward her as Mavka sprinkled the powder over her. Sorin came closer to her and to Shaye, who was sitting beside her. The Fate grabbed them both and bright light filled the house. When it faded, he found that they were in a different room. This one was spacious and sunny, with flowers blooming all around them. The smell of jasmine filled the air, warm and inviting.

"Welcome, Your Majesty." The tall, thin woman in front of them bowed deeply. Her appearance was like the Fate that had been in front of them, with the same, white-streaked hair and high cheekbones. Only now, she had clouded white eyes where they had been hollow before, and her mouth was free of the fog. Her complexion was clear, and milky white. She was in a beautiful glittering gown, unlike the tattered, bloodied one she had worn moments ago.

"My name is Lachtori. I am the one who sees what is to come."

Sorin took in the scene around them, still stunned by the sudden change, "Your sister, Clothsari... What happened to her? Who did this to you both?"

"The dark ones came as soon as night fell, cloaked in black magic so powerful that even I had not seen them coming. My sister and I had been waiting for you... For both of you." She gestured to Shaye and bowed to her as well. It was a deep bow, one typically given to royalty.

She straightened. "What they did not count on was my reserved magic. The young always think they know everything. I may be what one would call *ancient* but that only means I have a few tricks up my sleeve."

"So, this is your..." Shaye looked too shocked to speak.

"My mind. Yes. I have called you here so that I may give you what you seek."

She waved a steady hand, and suddenly the room faded away. In its place, a glittering cave appeared. They were now surrounded by crystals and a clear pool of water. "What you seek lies not far from here. My sister and I have kept an eye on it for you." She winked a clouded eye. "It will not go easily; beware the trials ahead. Like others before you, you must be tested and found worthy."

Sorin bowed to her. "Thank you Lachtori. And with all my heart, I am terribly sorry we did not get here sooner. To save you and your sister."

"Thank you for your kindness, King Sorin. I am afraid you have a long fight ahead of you. Stay vigilant and protect one another." She gestured to Shaye who bowed to her as well.

Sorin took Shaye's hand in his, giving it a gentle, reassuring squeeze.

"What will you do now?" Shaye asked, choking back tears.

"I will take my sister's body to Atropani so that we may complete her final resting rites. May the Mother carry you both safely through your quest."

The cave faded away and Sorin and Shaye found themselves back in the dark, crooked house. Lachtori stood before them, her mouth covered once again by the fog and her clouded eyes gone. She bowed, her way of telling them that they were done there. It was time to move on.

CHAPTER TWENTY-THREE

Sorin

T*hey did not have to* venture as far as he had expected. Once they helped Lachtori wrap her sister's body in a shroud and lay it safely on a small wagon, she bid them a silent farewell. In just a short ride, they had come to the narrow entrance of a cave. It appeared so suddenly that Sorin thought maybe it was another mirage like the one he had seen in Lachtori's mind. Mavka put a hand to her heart before entering. A sign of respect for what they were about to do.

The others looked nervously at the cave, unsure of what they were about to find in there. After their meeting with Lachtori, they described what they had seen in the vision, and Mavka had assured them that she knew exactly where the relic was hidden. There were only two caves near the Fate's cottage, and only one of those was rumored to have an entire cavern made of crystals.

Sorin could not stop thinking about the warning from Lachtori. The Stave would not be so easy to obtain, and he hated not knowing exactly what lay ahead of them. Especially with an enemy who knew they were coming. *Protect one another*. It had been her final warning to them.

"Sorin, I have a bad feeling about this." Shaye hadn't left his side since they departed from the cottage. She had removed her jacket when she noticed some of the Fate's blood on it. Her white blouse was belted and accented her waist, reminding him once again that she was not the little girl he had saved in the palace anymore.

She was looking at him expectantly. They were all on edge now. "You and me both. Just be on guard. Oh, and here." He handed her a small, jeweled dagger with the king's crest on it. "Just in case." He smirked, noting the blush on Shaye's cheeks as he did so.

The cave was vacant and damp. He could hear water dripping in one of the nearby caverns. It was hard to imagine his father here, in this dark cave, hiding away the relic that was key in his plans for change. *I guess we're not so different after all, father.* Sorin was here for change too. He needed to set things right and then he needed to fix this shattered kingdom. Needed to do right by *all* its people.

Mavka led them through the cave, sure of herself and of where Lachtori claimed they would find the Stave. He could feel the tension of his companions, ready for a fight. They would not be ambushed again like they had been with the Naga and the fog. Shaye walked beside him. He had felt a shift between them since that moment in the library, but he tried to focus on the task at hand.

They continued deeper into the cavern until they entered a room filled with awe-inspiring crystals. There was a shallow pool below, and just beyond stood the Stave of Leto. Just as Lachtori had shown them. It was like it had been waiting for them, positioned proudly, leaning on a flat, silken rock. It was slightly longer than a broadsword, and thin with a twisted knot of wood at the top. Sorin's breath caught in his throat when he saw that it was split, revealing splintered wood where its other half had been removed. Anywhere else and he would have overlooked it as fire kindling. But here, under the fluorescent light of the crystals, it called to him. One half of the Stave.

"What happened to it?" Bron wrinkled his brow beside Sorin.

"It's been broken in half." Mavka whispered in disbelief. "Where is the other piece?"

Sorin removed his weapons and jacket. "It doesn't matter right now. We retrieve this half first, then worry about the rest."

He moved to get into the pool of water, but a small hand stopped him. "Careful, Your Majesty," Mavka's voice echoed softly. "It will not allow you to take it without a fight."

"Allow me to go, Sir." Anik volunteered, already removing his boots.

"No, I've brought us this far, it is my risk to take." He kicked off his boots. "I've always been a better swimmer than you anyways," he added jokingly, though no one laughed.

Shaye put a hand on his arm. "Sorin, Mavka is right. This feels too easy."

He smiled, brushing off her concern as he inched closer to the water. Shaye walked at his side, dagger in hand. Bron stood with Anik, surveying the dark corners of the arched walls. This was it, there was no time to waste, they needed the Stave and they needed it now. He felt a tug as if it were calling to him.

He neared the water's edge, but the moment his foot hit the water, the cavern quaked. Shaye shouted to him, grabbing at his sleeve, but it was too late. He felt her fingers slip away from him as a strong hand grabbed his leg and pulled him under. Ice cold water filled his nose and he thrashed in a panic. He could hear distant shouting, but there was nothing he could do except allow himself to be pulled deeper into the glistening pool.

Reaching for his knife, he attempted to slash at whatever monster was drowning him. He had spent years at the docks with the fishermen and time as a boy swimming in the ponds around Asterion. He had always considered himself a strong swimmer, but nothing could match whatever it was pulling him to a watery grave.

He shut his eyes and thought of Shaye. *This cannot be how it ends.* When he opened his eyes, he saw the creature that was fighting hard to drown him. What he had not expected to see was a beautiful, dark-skinned woman coated in golden scales. Her black hair swirled around them both and he could have sworn he saw her smile.

Her voice echoed in his head, though her mouth never moved. *Come with me, Sorin of Asterion. Let go of it all and you will find peace in the deep.*

NO. He kicked at her and tried to roll away from her sharp grasp. There seemed to be no escaping her. She smiled again, flashing white, pointed teeth at him. She reminded him of the sirens he had seen in the paintings at the Winter Palace.

Her voice rang in his mind. *Close, young King. Too bad you have failed before you have even begun. My master wants you dead, and I must obey.*

Realization hit him then. *Not a siren. A Ceasg.* A mermaid who, if legends were right, would grant wishes to whomever captured her. Before she could react, he undid the baldrick strapped around his chest and swung it around her neck. She let out a piercing cry as he pulled them both to the surface.

When they emerged from the water, they were on the other side of the pool; the Stave laid within his reach. The Ceasg wailed and thrashed under his hold, but he refused to release her. Holding tight, he dragged her onto the smooth, cold stones. "Three wishes, if I am correct."

She stilled. Her scales glistened in the light of the crystals; her onyx-colored hair was tangled and wet. He heard the others gasp from across the pool at the sight of him and the Ceasg. He heard Shaye sob with relief. When he looked back at his friends, she was on her knees with Bron's arms wrapped around her, holding her back from the water.

"I will make you a deal." Sorin began to release her from his hold. "You grant me *one* wish and I will release you to live your life as you please."

Her ebony eyes went wide in surprise. "A trick. Like the dark ones before you played on me."

Sorin had a faint idea of who she might be referring to... The Nefari. "No tricks here. We simply need to take that relic with us."

The Ceasg thought for a moment. Part of him worried she would plunge him back into that water, until golden dust erupted from her hands, and in the blink of an eye he was holding the Stave. Or what was left of it...

"It is done," she said scornfully. "Now *release* me." Her accent was thick. It was clear she was not from Asterion.

"I wish that you would be free as long as you live."

Sparks went ablaze in the cavern, and he heard his friends on the other side of the pool gasp. When the light subsided, a woman was standing tall before him. The Ceasg had shed her scaled tail and stood now on two legs in an elaborate golden dress embroidered with the finest silk. On her head she wore a golden headpiece, detailed with crystals from the cave.

"Are we free to go?" he asked, unsure of what to do next.

She nodded, staring at him in awe. As he turned back toward the water, ready to escape this horrible cave, she called out to him, "Why would you do that? Why set me free when you could have bid me to do whatever you pleased?"

"No one in this world, or the next, deserves to live a life in servitude to another."

He prepared himself to get back into the cold water, but she spoke again, "The ones who trapped me here, they will hunt you down, you know."

"Trust me, we know, but we'll be ready." Sorin adjusted his baldrick, strapping the Stave into place with it.

"You will need help," she offered, wading into the water where he stood. She held out her hand to him, still glittering with shimmering dust, a sign of her magic.

"If you are offering, we will take all of the help we can get. But please, know that you owe me nothing. And the big one there," he pointed to Bron, "he snores like a bear."

The Ceasg chuckled. It sounded like waves crashing into the shore, "Bears don't scare me and neither do the men who put me here. I will help you of my own free will. It is my decision, and it is final."

Sorin took her hand in his, shaking it in acceptance of her offer to help. She held her head high, "I am Ingemar."

"It is nice to meet you, Ingemar."

They crossed the pool, back to his companions. Shaye was pale and wet. She had jumped in after him to rescue him from a murky death before Bron had pulled her back to shore. No matter how unfruitful her efforts had been, Sorin could not help but feel gratitude toward her. Bron had done what he had instructed; he had kept her safe.

When they reached the shore, Shaye threw her arms around him. "Don't you ever go in alone like that again, do you understand?" When she pulled back, she hit him in the chest.

Pulling her back into his arms, he smiled. "I understand."

Once they made their way back into the mouth of the cavern, Ingemar told them her story. She explained how she had been captured by a group of men with hands as black as coal. They had only one wish, for her to guard the relic no matter who came looking for it, no matter how long it took.

She hadn't understood it at the time, for they had split it in two before taking their leave. But she had been bound, as is the nature of her kind. She had not known who they were, only that they needed the Stave to remain here.

They made camp in the mouth of the cave, Sorin and Bron questioning her well into the night. They needed to know every little detail about the men who had taken her, no matter how small and insignificant it seemed. She was happy to share what she knew, but there were no clues as to where the Nefari were making their camp or who was leading them. She did not know how many of them there were or what they were planning next. Sorin shook his head in frustration; the Nefari were proving themselves to be a formidable opponent.

It was Mavka who caught their attention when she asked, "Why do you think the Nefari left the broken piece behind? Why not keep the pieces together or turn it to ash? It seems careless of them to leave it for us to find."

Bron agreed, "She's right, and careless hasn't been their style up to this point." He kicked at the dirt. "Even with the Fates; they deliberately left the carnage for us to find, like they were taunting us."

It was a question Sorin had asked himself since the moment they had laid eyes on the broken Stave. But he did not have an answer.

Ingemar poked at the ground with a stick. Her hands still shimmered like faint scales, lingering through the magic that had transformed her. She was thoughtful for a moment before she spoke, "There was a tale our elders used to tell. Of a siren king in the Eastern Isles. His kingdom had been vast and the envy of many. They had prospered in the safety of their kingdom under the sea. Until a powerful Sea-Witch amassed enough power to try to steal the trident from him."

Sorin leaned forward with his arms resting on his legs, lost in the tale as she continued, "Though she failed in the attack, the King had worried that his people could not hold up against the Witch's army. The King broke the trident. He did this to prevent it from being used by his enemies. Even if it meant never again holding its power for himself. He did not fear the loss of it because he believed that one day, his daughter, who had been hidden away, would become strong enough to piece it back together.

Destroying the trident and its power had only been a temporary sacrifice. By breaking it into shards they were able to keep it from the Sea-Witch's grasp. Perhaps we are seeing something similar here. The Nefari have broken the Stave to release their dark power beyond the forest and into the rest of Asterion. Until they become powerful enough to put it back together and use it against their enemies."

It made sense, Sorin thought. If they could not use it yet, then it would have been safer to split it in two, keeping one piece with them while putting the other one in a guarded location. Which only meant that they were not done with this piece of the relic. He touched their half of the Stave and power vibrated from it, even in its current state.

It was strange to think that such an ordinary-looking piece of wood could have such magic within it. He kicked at the dirt in front of him. The ease that had surrounded them earlier was gone now, replaced with tension.

Mavka whispered to her moths, "Okay, okay, I'll ask her." She looked to Ingemar, who was eyeing the small girl with curiosity and good humor. "Ingemar, we were wondering, what is it like where you're from?"

Ingemar thought for a moment before replying, "It feels strange to answer your question. My people have been in hiding for so long... But I can tell you that it is the most beautiful place in this world. The waters are always clear and sparkling. Much like your Asterion, magic lives within it. We are a peaceful people. Too much danger awaits us on the shore, so we must protect one another. Fierce fighters, truly fierce." Wild beauty danced in her eyes.

Mavka sighed and leaned against Bron. "I wish I could see it. I should very much like to see everything."

Sorin cut in, "Then you will. We will take you to Aramoor first, so you can shop in the trade district and-"

Shaye interrupted excitedly, "And taste Rolland's cooking! Oh, and I'll introduce you to Brina; the two of you would really like each other." They all laughed.

Bron took a turn, "And I will take you to a ball."

They were all stunned, staring wide-eyed as they tried to picture Bron, of all people, at a ball, with the forest girl on his arm.

"What?" He threw his hands up in defense. "I like a good ball as much as the next guy."

Everyone laughed hysterically, but Mavka whispered, "I would love that. All of that."

Bron took a long swig from the flask and Mavka yawned. Storytime was over.

Sometime later in the night, Sorin awoke to a familiar voice. It was calling out to him to help, but when he looked around, his companions were sleeping peacefully. He tried to shake the feeling and laid back down on his bedroll, but as soon as he shut his eyes, he heard it again. This time the call was more urgent, pleading for him to help. It was Elijah. He would have known that voice anywhere. In an instant, Sorin was up, sword in hand. He did not bother with his boots as he walked slowly toward the mouth of the cave. Elijah's voice called out from the forest, pleading for Sorin to help him.

Please, Sorin, I'm hurt real bad. Sorin...

The hair on Sorin's arms stood and his heart raced. *I must go to him.* "Elijah! Wait there, I'm coming for you." Before Sorin could step foot outside of the cave, a hand pulled him back. It was Shaye. She was standing wide-eyed, her fingers held fast to his shirtsleeve.

"Shaye, what are you doing? He needs me, let go." He pushed her hand away and moved to help his friend. Instead of a hand, this time he was met with a force that knocked him back into the cave. He spun on his heel, anger seething from him. What were they doing? Elijah was out there alone, and he needed help.

Ingemar stood, hands extended as gold dust flurried in the air. "Your Majesty, no one is out there."

"He's there! I can hear him. Can't you hear him Bron? Anik?" He looked to his friends for assistance, but they just stared back at him bleary-eyed.

Mavka let out a yawn. "She's right your Majesty, it is only a trick. A very *mean* trick."

Sorin, brother, please, I'm cold, I want to go home, Elijah called to him again; Sorin turned on Ingemar. "Release the wall, *now*, that is an order from your *King.*"

"With all due respect, King Sorin, you are not *my* King. And I will not allow you, or anyone else, to be harmed by whatever dark magic lurks beyond these rocky walls." She held her magic, Sorin was no match.

Shaye touched his cheek tenderly. "Sorin, look, *really look.* What do you see?"

He wiped the sweat from his brow and gazed out of the cave, in the direction of Elijah's call. Despair filled him when he saw a dense, black fog weaving in and out of the trees. Elijah wasn't there. He was gone, taken by the fog, and now it was here, taunting him. He sank to his knees, leaning into Shaye as she stood by his side, stroking his hair.

He turned to her, burying his head against her legs and sobbed, "I'm sorry. I'm so sorry." They stayed like that for a while, him crying for the loss of his friend, Shaye running her hands along his hair.

Once everyone had settled back down, he was able to drift back to sleep. Shaye had moved her bedroll closer to his. He imagined she was afraid to leave him alone after what had almost happened. If he had left the cave, the man-eating fog would have taken him, just as it had taken Elijah, just as it had tried to take Shaye on the cliff. Ingemar assured them that her magic would hold through the night, preventing anything from entering the cave while they slept. He was suddenly incredibly grateful for Ingemar, who had tried to drown him just hours earlier.

When they awoke in the morning there was desperation in the air. They knew a few things for sure: The dark Magi were extremely powerful, and they were enemies of the crown, ready to cross any line to get what they wanted. He spent the morning apologizing to his friends for the night before. He had put them and the entire country in danger by being so naive. And he had insulted Ingemar in the process. They were all very gracious, promising that there were no hard feelings, nothing he needed to apologize for.

"You know I would have done the same, brother." Bron patted Sorin on the back before mounting Altivo.

Sorin pulled Shaye aside once they had finished packing. They were headed back to the Palace to decide what their next steps would be.

"If you want to leave, then I understand. We are dealing with something much bigger here than I thought. If you left now, no one would blame you."

"None of us had any idea what we were walking into. But I am here, so I plan to see this through." She grabbed his hand and he relaxed at her touch.

"When we get back to the Palace we need to talk."

Shaye bit her lip and nodded, "Of course."

The ride back to the Winter Palace went much faster than the journey to the cave. The horses were glad to be in the stables again and Shaye took the time to give each of them an apple in reward for the journey. Sorin loved the way she doted on Finn and how he would catch her in private conversation with the gelding.

Back in the palace everyone was quiet; it seemed to be a pattern of theirs after each challenge they faced, each lost in thought. Ingemar had kept her word and insisted on coming back with them. Against Sorin's protests she claimed that she would not be swayed.

Bron offered to fetch them dinner and bounded off with Mavka glued to his side. She was infatuated with Bron and his human-like mannerisms. Sorin could hear her pleading with him to explain to her what a tavern was as they ventured to the kitchen.

"Shaye, could we talk?" Sorin needed to talk to her while they finally had a moment alone.

"Of course." She smiled sweetly at him. Even with dirty clothes and dirt on her face from the long journey, she was a wonder. It was becoming increasingly impossible to deny his attraction to her, especially with the memory of her lips on his lingering in his mind.

He pulled her into the parlor and shut the door, keeping her hands in his. Taking a deep breath, he prepared to tell her about the night of the uprising. He wanted her to know that he was not like his father... That even as a boy, he had believed in a peaceful transition. Sorin had had every intention of sounding the alarm that night and giving the courtiers a chance at escaping or, at the very least, the opportunity to defend themselves. But before he could find the words, there was an urgent banging at the palace door.

CHAPTER TWENTY-FOUR

Shaye

A loud banging at the palace doors made Shaye jump. She could hear panicked shouting from out in the entryway. Who could possibly have followed them to the safety of the palace grounds? Mavka had assured them that no one would dare venture here, and Bron and Anik had been vigilant in their patrols.

She followed Sorin into the entryway. He had not let go of her hand yet, and she did not pull away. Bron and Anik were already there with their swords drawn. The banging continued until Ingemar opened the door. A night breeze blew in and, on the threshold, stood a man in a deep burgundy cloak, his face hidden beneath the hood. The stranger had no weapons on him that Shaye could see, and he was trembling where he stood.

The man fell to the ground in a heap, hood sliding from his face, and it was then that Shaye saw him. It was a face that had appeared in so many of her dreams, though he had been years younger then. She couldn't believe what she was seeing; the face of the one person in this world, before Brina, that she had truly allowed herself to trust.

Shaye gasped in recognition and whispered the name she had not spoken out loud in a very long time, "Bastian."

She released Sorin's hand and ran to Bastian, reaching him just as he fell to the ground. His face was bloody and swollen. Something had done quite a number on him. She didn't know what to say or do. It had been so long since she had seen him... Up until this moment she feared he had died during the Winter Solstice. His dark brown eyes locked onto Shaye's before he lost consciousness.

Shaye turned to Sorin, pleading with him, "Sorin, please, help him."

Sorin rushed to her where she held Bastian's head in her lap and signaled to the others to help carry him to the parlor. They lifted him carefully, carrying him to the dimly lit room and laying him on the chaise lounge. Her friends gave her puzzled looks but she ignored them, trying to sort through her own thoughts. She sent Mavka to the kitchen to fetch water as Bron and Anik left to check the perimeter for any lingering threat. Something had certainly attacked him out there, though they had no idea where he had come from and how he had made his way to the palace. Shaye had always had trouble believing in fate, but it seemed too big of a coincidence that he would appear here after all this time.

"Shaye, who is this man?" Sorin had a look of genuine concern on his face.

"His name is Bastian. We grew up together." She gestured around them. "Here in the palace."

Bastian stirred on the couch and fluttered his eyes open. Passing quickly over the others, his gaze found Shaye, and he moved to get up, struggling.

She stopped him, "You need to rest. Here, lay down." She

propped a pillow up for his head so he could lay at an incline. Mavka returned with water, eyeing him warily.

"Thank you." His voice was hoarse, and he winced as he moved for the water, taking it in his gloved hands. He wore an expensive looking cloak, but the rest of his clothes looked worn and tired.

"Bastian, what are you doing here?" Shaye was in such disbelief at his appearance that she could not process the endless list of questions running through her mind. It had been over a decade since she had last laid eyes on him. His dark hair shined like the night sky, despite the rest of his appearance. It was longer than she remembered, falling nearly to his shoulders. He was tall and lean and incredibly handsome. She blushed at the thought and looked around to make sure her friends did not notice her flushed face. She looked to Sorin, feeling a strange bit of guilt for thinking that way.

"After the dark night of the Solstice, I fled with others to the west, where a ship was waiting to take us to Skag. I have been there for the last twelve years, making a living from hunting and selling pelts in the mountains. But then rumors began to flood into their shores and I wanted to see for myself if they were true. I returned only days ago, sure that I would return to find the rumors false. Unfortunately, I was wrong." He winced, "I wasn't prepared for them to be *this* true; I had a run in with a *Black Shuck*."

"By the looks of it he gave it to you good." Bron laughed from the doorway. "All clear out there, whatever attacked him is long gone. Not even a track left behind."

Shaye felt all eyes on her. She knew Sorin was waiting for her word that Bastian could be trusted, but she honestly had no idea; her childhood with him felt like another lifetime. *She* had certainly changed. She had been a child when they last saw one another; now here she was trying to save an entire country with a king she was starting to care for, against her better judgment.

Whether or not Bastian was telling the truth, it would be better to keep him close until they figured it out. There were things lurking beyond the palace walls, and she did not want to risk turning him away alone, and defenseless toward that danger. She gave Sorin a curt nod.

Bastian fell asleep shortly after, and Shaye and the rest of the group retired to the dining room for a late dinner. The table had been set and was laid out with an impressive spread. Bron and Anik had gone hunting. And Ingemar, with the help of a curious Mavka, had prepared what felt like a feast after spending so long on the road.

Along the table there were figs, apples, and venison meat pie. The room smelled amazing, and Shaye felt a sudden pang of homesickness, thinking of the supper the Erlands must be sitting down at their own table to eat. She wondered if they were worried, Shaye had not yet been able to send word to them and she prayed they would know in their hearts that she was okay.

Bron sat across from her, plate piled high. "I'll say what we're all thinking: His showing up here today can't be a coincidence." He bit into a small apple, eating half of it in that one bite.

Shaye bit her lip, wondering how she could explain this to them best. "We were close growing up. He was my only ally here when we were children. But it has been over a decade since we last saw each other. I'm sorry I just... I don't know what to think yet."

Sorin cut in, "What we can be sure of is, if he *was* attacked by a Black Shuck, then that means the Nefari could be nearby. Black Shuck are demon dogs, notorious companion creatures, more often than not they are sent to do their master's bidding. My guess is that it is no coincidence that one was found so close to the palace. They may know that we have recovered half of the Stave."

"If that piece of the Stave was so important to them, then wouldn't they have come for it by now?" Bron sounded confident, but the look in his eyes told Shaye otherwise.

Ingemar was the one to say what Shaye was too afraid of voicing out loud, "Maybe they already have." They all looked toward the door, just beyond the hall to where Bastian was laying.

It was hard for Shaye to believe, but his story about Skag and his coming here... It was all too much to wrap her head around. All she knew was that she had to talk to him, and soon, for her own piece of mind and for her friends. The last thing she wanted to do was put any of them in danger.

Once dinner was over and the table had been cleared, Anik and Bron left for another perimeter check. Shaye knew there would be countless more to follow that night. Everyone was on edge, and there would likely be little sleep for any of them tonight. Mavka showed Ingemar to her room, eagerly questioning her about living in the sea. Sorin lingered. Shaye could tell he wanted to speak with her, but she desperately wanted to check in on Bastian. She would give Sorin all the time in the world after that was done.

"Shaye, I really need a moment." The exhaustion was evident in his bloodshot eyes, and she could see his weariness in the way he was leaning on the chair. She wanted to reassure him, to hold his hand and tell him it was all going to be okay. But she could not promise that yet, not until she spoke with Bastian alone and figured out if this was, in fact, all a coincidence.

"I know, but can it wait just a little longer? I just need to talk to Bastian quickly. If I can just talk to him alone, maybe I can sort this whole thing out."

"Shaye, we still don't know that he can be trusted. I'm not comfortable leaving you alone with him yet."

Shaye understood his concern, but she knew Bastian would not talk openly in front of the King, especially when that king was the son of Allerick. She put a hand to his chest, "I can handle myself and you are just a shout away. I'll be fine, I promise." She added with a smirk, "And I have this." She patted Sorin's jeweled dagger that she now wore at her side. She had replaced her old one with it, liking the way it felt on her hip.

He looked as if he would argue with her, but instead nodded. "Will you come find me when you're done?"

"Of course." She took her hand from him and smiled softly. It was obvious today had gotten to him, and as reluctant as she was to admit it, she was worried about him. She would make things quick with Bastian and then give Sorin all the time he needed to tell her what was on his mind.

Shaye entered the parlor which was lit only by a small lantern on the side table where Bastian laid. He was asleep with a peaceful look on his battered face. Sweat was beaded along his brow, but the color had come back to his cheeks. One of his eyes was swollen, but his wounds had been cleaned up by Mavka. The same smelly salve she had used on Bron was smeared on the more severe cuts. It was lucky for them that the Forest Dweller had joined them on their journey, and Shaye had a sick feeling that they would need more of her healing expertise in the days to come.

She wanted to reach out to him, to touch him, to see if he was real or if this was just another one of her dreams. But she hesitated. Instead, she sat on the floor by his side, thinking of the last time she had seen him. The memories of that night were difficult to revisit. She had exiled them to her nightmares only, avoiding them as much as she could when she was awake. Being here with him now was surreal. Instead, she conjured up happier memories, like the first one she had of him.

"You probably don't remember the first time we met," she chuckled, half talking to herself and half hoping he could hear her. "I was in the school yard. Nanny Jin was looking for me, ready to whip my hide for stealing tarts from the kitchen. My hiding spot of choice that day was behind a particularly scandalous statue. Remember how much the old queen hated those naked statues King Idor would commission? Anyway, Ivar, that little jerk, had spotted me and had run off to tell Nanny where I was hiding."

Bastian laughed, his eyes still closed. "I took one look at your face and knew you didn't deserve what was coming to you, that you were far too clever to deserve the lashing that was sure to come when they found you. So I used a spell to call the wind, knocking him right on his ass. He pummeled me afterwards for it."

Shaye laughed too, "But he'd been so focused on you, that he forgot to tell Nanny where I was." She sighed, "You always looked out for me. Even if it meant taking a hit for me."

"Seems not much has changed." His eyes were open now; he was gazing up at Shaye. She could not believe the beautiful man laying before her now was the same lanky boy from her past. She could still see the boy that she once loved in those dark eyes.

Her voice was barely a whisper, "Bass, what happened that night?"

Frustration flashed across his face, so quickly that she thought maybe she had imagined it. Bastian sat up now, wincing from his injuries which were still trying to heal themselves with the aid of the salve. His shirt was torn in the front so that Mavka could apply the bandages, and Shaye could not help but stare. Bastian was not as broad or muscular as Sorin, but he had a strong, lean body.

Bastian brought her gaze back to his face. "I looked for you. We had been separated by the crowd in the ballroom. Do you not remember any of this?"

Shaye shook her head. "It's too painful. I see that night in my dreams, but you are always so far away. No matter how hard I fight to get to you, you're always out of reach."

He reached a shaky hand up to cup her face, his thumb grazed her lips gently. "We got out Shaye. We survived and lived. And once again, fate has brought us back together."

Her heart raced at his touch. It was like lightning coursing through her veins and suddenly she could see it. Her vision began to cloud, and her mind went back to that night. She saw it as clearly as if she were there now. King Allerick's men were cutting down anyone in their path, both men and women. Her uncle, across the room, tried to use his magic but it had failed him that night. It was failing all the Magi in the room, and their faces were a picture of pure terror and confusion. Then a hand, *his* hand. But the eyes were wrong, they were not supposed to be brown like Bastian's... They should be blue...

She pulled away from Bastian and shook her head. Everything felt hazy and she struggled to push the memory away once again. In her dreams they were always blue, or maybe her damaged mind had gotten that wrong. Bass had always protected her, so who else, if not him, would have saved her that night? "I thought you were dead."

"I'm here, Shaye, and I'm never leaving you behind again." He looked at her with fierce intensity. "When I heard about the relic and what was happening here, something inside of me urged me to come back home, and here you were. I can hardly believe it."

Home. That is what it had been for them, here in Brenmar, in the Winter Palace. They had been home for one another, steady presences in each other's lives, in a place where they were considered outcasts by everyone else. He had to be telling the truth; something inside her *had* to believe that.

"Will you help us then?"

"For you, Shaye? Anything."

After their talk, Shaye walked Bastian to the room he would be staying in, not far from her own. It had been rough getting him up the stairs, but she was sure he would feel better in the morning, after a good night's rest. They said their goodnights and then she followed the deep purple carpet down to Sorin's room. She only had to knock once before the door opened.

"You came." He sounded relieved. Sorin was still in his breeches, but his tunic was open at the top, revealing his tanned chest. Shaye's breath caught in her throat at the sight of him.

"I talked to Bastian... I believe him and think he can help. I know it will take time for you all to trust him as I do, but I just need you to give him a chance." Shaye stepped into the room and Sorin shut the door behind them. She didn't mind; she had been alone with him before. She knew by now, after weeks of traveling together, after the moments they had shared leading up to this point, Sorin was no threat to her. Their arms brushed as she passed him.

"I understand that the two of you have a past but..."

"Please, Sorin, trust me. He is on our side; he wants to protect his home. The blight helps no one, human or Magi. And his magic was always stronger than mine. He was advanced in his studies. If anyone can help, then it's him."

"Okay, I will agree to give him a chance, but we need to keep our guard up right now. We don't know who the Nefari are, we only know that they are Magi." He gestured for her to sit and poured them both a glass of red wine. He sat beside her on the bed, close enough that their legs touched.

He looked apprehensive now, and took a big swig from his

glass. "There's no right way to say this so I'm just going to come out with it. I have waited for you to say something first, but you haven't yet, and maybe you don't remember, but I feel like you need to know... because the longer I go without saying anything, the more it feels like I'm keeping things from you."

Shaye's brow furrowed; it was hard to follow him when he was babbling. "Sorin... what is it that you want to tell me exactly?" She smiled to try to calm his nerves.

"I was there. That night. I mean, I was *here*."

"In the palace?"

"Yes, my father had brought me along. My job was to stand back, observe only."

"Observe the massacre." She felt dizzy at the revelation that he had taken part in what had happened that night.

"Shaye, please believe me, I had no idea what was going to happen. They had talked of taking out the guards only. Of overpowering them and arresting the old king and his family. The relic had already been put into play at that point, so the Magi were no longer a threat. I thought they were all to be tried and *exiled*. And maybe that is what my father had intended, but then the doors locked, and all hell broke loose."

Shaye fought back the bile rising in her throat as she recalled those first moments of panic, when the courtiers realized they had been surrounded. *Trapped*. Like pigs to slaughter.

Sorin's voice trembled, "I knew immediately what I needed to do. I decided at that moment that I would run to the nearest entrance guarded by my father's men. I would slip past them and unlock the other doors, allowing for an escape route. But then I saw you."

"Me?" She could barely speak, could barely think. The walls of the room seemed to close in around her and it was getting difficult to breathe.

"Yes. You were standing there, frozen in fear. You were not running or screaming like the others. Instead, you just stood, tears streaming down your face. Then you looked at me with those pleading, startling, golden eyes, and something inside me demanded I go to you. I made a choice. I chose to grab you first, and then run. I don't know why, but in that moment everything inside of me was *screaming* to get you away from there. I grabbed your hand, and we ran."

Sorin's hands shook as he continued. "At first, I led us toward the main entrance, the one I had planned to unlock. But there were too many people, too much danger... Danger I did not want to drag you towards. So, we went out the back, slipping through a servant's entrance. And I know you may never forgive me. I cannot even forgive myself for leaving the others behind. But my instincts were telling me that it was *you* I had been there to save. That fate *demanded* it. I thought I could get you out of there and go back for the others, but by the time I returned, it was over. I was too late." He put his head in his hands.

Blue eyes. She had seen them in her dreams, deep blue eyes and a boy who had pulled her away from the nightmare. *Brown.* The word echoed in her mind. She felt faint and could not think straight. The words of Atropani echoed in her mind, *Do not trust the honeyed words of men.* But which man the seer had been referring to, she did not know. She closed her eyes tight, trying to remember. No they had been brown, she was sure of it. She was also sure she was going to be sick. Everything was going dark, shadows closed in all around Shaye, ready to devour her, like the fog in the forest. She tried to stand, she needed air, needed to clear her head.

Shaye. Shaye! She could hear Sorin calling her name. It was too far away though, like Bastian's voice had been in her dreams. And as she drifted into nothingness it was Bastian's eyes that she saw before fading into oblivion.

CHAPTER TWENTY-FIVE

Sorin

S *orin stayed by her side* the entire night. When she passed out, he had rushed to find Mavka, trusting the dweller to use her herbal magic to bring Shaye back to consciousness. Mavka assured him that Shaye would be fine, that it had only been what looked like an attack of the nerves. Shaye had fainted, and he felt sick to his stomach knowing that he had been the cause of it. Maybe he had made a mistake telling her, dredging up old memories.

He knew how Shaye struggled in the night. Throughout their journey, she had often called out for someone to help her, waking with sobs. Although she had done her best to hide her trembling hands and quick, shallow breaths, he had seen the signs. He had seen the symptoms before, in men home from battle. That sort of trauma never leaves you; your mind and your body will not let it. Preventing you from forgetting, from letting your guard down.

The truth had felt so important to him that he had not considered what it might drudge up. He set down the book he was reading and moved his chair closer to her bedside. Too afraid to move her, he had tucked her into his own bed. He pulled the blankets over her, tucking them in gently around her. Mavka had left around midnight, but he had stayed by her side all night, drifting off to sleep occasionally, in an oversized gaudy green chair. He had awoken this morning at dawn and decided to pick up *The Final Judgment,* once more.

It struck him as odd how closely he related to the brothers from the story. He could relate to being thrown into this new world but still haunted by the memory of the old. Their fore-fathers had destroyed their home in battle, forcing the brothers to pick up the pieces. They had been angry, hurt, and hopeless, looking for a way to right the wrongs of the past and start a new life. They had been given a second chance to do better, *be* better. The relics had been gifts and a test of their worthiness to live in peace here in Asterion. Something he now faced in a different sort of way.

Maybe his test was not that of setting things back to the way they were, though. The Nefari were the real threat here, not the broken relic. If he could seek out the Nefari and stop them from whatever they had planned, then maybe there would be no need to put the Stave back together at all.

He was King now, with the ability to choose who was granted power and favor. With Shaye's help, he could keep history from repeating itself with the Magi. It was a dreamer's way of thinking, he knew. But if the Magi could find a way to follow rules and regulations the way the Guilds did...

"Sorin?" Shaye sat up, her hair such a disheveled mess that he had to suppress a smirk.

"You had us scared there for a minute." He dared to put a hand to her cheek, caressing it lightly.

"I'm so sorry, it feels like it was all a dream." She grabbed her head in pain and Sorin hurried to hand her some water. She drank deeply and went on, "The last thing I remember clearly is sitting beside Bastian. We were reminiscing about the day we met." She groaned in pain, "I'm sorry, my head is just pounding."

"I'm so sorry, Shaye."

"There is nothing for you to apologize for. It's been a long few days and I just needed some rest, that's all."

He studied her face for a moment. "I'll fetch Mavka to help you with that headache and get you something to eat."

"Could you send for Bastian as well?"

Sorin nodded hesitantly and left to find Mavka first. Nightmares and panic attacks were one thing, but memory loss was another. What if her coming back here, coming face-to-face with someone from her childhood, and the stress of the day, had stirred up more than they realized?

Mavka wasn't in her room, so he ventured to the kitchens in search of her. When he walked into the deep stone room, he was surprised to find Bastian there sharing a cup of tea with the Forest Dweller. They were laughing as he tried to explain to her that spoons were used for scooping and stirring food, *not* for making music.

Mavka had never been around humans and had never seen their inventions. For as long as she had lived, which Sorin gathered had been quite long, she had never been able to interact with the human world like this. It gave her a child-like fascination and obsession to learn more about the wonders it had to offer. He looked forward to inviting her back to Aramoor like they had talked about, when all of this was over, to explore the city with Shaye and the others. If Shaye chose to stay, that is.

Sorin cleared his throat to let them know he was there. Mavka leapt up from her chair, "How is she?"

"Awake but foggy. Would you mind taking her something to help with a headache?"

"I know just the thing!" She jumped up, tossed some

strange-looking flowers into a teacup, and skipped from the room.

"Thank The Mother she's okay." Bastian set his tea down gently.

"Mavka filled you in?"

"She did. You know, Shaye has always been prone to bad nerves. It's not surprising that they've grown worse over the years." He leaned back in his seat as Sorin took up the chair across from him. "I mean, losing her parents so young, being subjected to the rigorous training from the Master Mages... and just as she was finally giving this place a chance, she was torn away from it. Forced to start over, alone again."

Sorin thought he heard a hint of pleasure when Bastian spoke of Shaye's misfortune. He brushed away the thought, blaming it on jealousy. Bastian took his cup to the sink and headed for the door. "I'll go check in on her, see if there's anything I can do to help."

Sorin sat at the small table for a while, contemplating Bastian and his interest in Shaye. Of course, there was a connection there. Shaye and Bastian were a big part of each other's pasts, but they weren't kids anymore. They had been apart for years and that was a lifetime of change; they had grown up, and Sorin could hardly assume she, or Bastian, were the same people after all this time. Especially after all that they had been through and witnessed.

Not to mention the timing and coincidence of Bastian showing up like this. Last night when Shaye had assured Sorin that she trusted Bastian, he had wanted to believe her. He needed her to know that he trusted her judgment and that her opinion mattered to him. What troubled Sorin now was that she had been fine when she had left him after dinner.

Now she was claiming that she could remember nothing past her talk with Bastian. Was the stress getting to her? There was no indication that something was wrong when she came to him. Whatever was affecting Shaye, it was bad. *Maybe Ingemar will have some ideas.*

Sorin walked through the palace gardens. The flowers that had once been beautiful were now overgrown and dead, a shadow of their former beauty. He could remember how meticulously kept these gardens were on the night of the Winter Solstice. The first signs of snow had been dusted from the shrubs and trees that had been sculpted into the shapes of magical creatures. Now they stood before him, bare and dying. Even the marble statues that once stood proud and bold were chipped and discolored. It was a tragedy in and of itself.

Sorin continued down to Brenmar Lake where Ingemar had been spending her spare time. She sat on a smooth flat rock, her tail was shining in the sunlight, in place of where her legs had been. She looked peaceful, swishing the golden scales around in the cool, clear water. Bron and Anik were nearby, hunting for small game. They were not sure how much longer they would be residing here in the Winter Palace; he had not decided yet. So, in the meantime, his friends did their best to prepare and make nights feel safe and comfortable. They all needed to find comfort wherever they could get it, he supposed.

"Ingemar. I'm sorry to intrude, but I was hoping we could talk."

Her dark skin glowed under the bright spring light, partially covered in the same beautiful scales that made up her tail. "Of course, young King." She gestured for him to join her.

Sorin removed his boots, rolling up his breeches, so he could dip his feet into the lake with her. "It's about Bastian."

"Ah, the young Magi, with the curious ability to appear from thin air." She raised a dark eyebrow. "You do not trust him?"

"No. I do not." He peered across the lake, wishing it could

give him some answers. "Am I using my better judgment here or am I letting my feelings for..." He trailed off, looking back at the Ceasg.

"Your 'feelings for Shaye,' you were going to say." A brilliant smile flashed across her face. "We see things. My people have a connection to the water, and the water never forgets. Its memory spans to the beginning of creation. And one thing the water has always taught me is *life for life*. The world is about balance. We see it in nature, in the circle of life. In the world of magic, to receive you must give, whether it be thanks, energy, or blood.

"Humans hold the same balance; for example, we have you and Shaye. Amid chaos, you made a choice to save a girl who had been alone in her life for so long, who had been left undefended. Maybe it was fate, maybe it had been The Mother herself who had urged you to save her. But the moment you did, your lives were connected. *You* became responsible for the life you had saved. Perhaps that force is what brought the two of you back together." She splashed a bit in the water, continuing while Sorin sat in thoughtful silence.

"Sorin, I know you can feel it deep in your bones. Whatever it may be, the water assures me that the two of you have a destiny far greater than that of any childhood crush. I cannot say whether Bastian is a threat, but I *can* tell you to tread lightly. There is something keeping him in the dark. So that I and the water cannot even see how he came to be here with us."

It was a lot to process. He had never told anyone about that night. Last night, alone with Shaye, had been the first time he had ever spoken of it out loud. He had been so focused on the mission at hand that he had not allowed himself to consider the coincidence that Shaye, of all people in this world, was the last of the Druid bloodline in Asterion record. That she was the one his mother and council had assured him was their only hope.

Perhaps magic had been so absent from his life, he had not really believed that the land itself held its own ancient magic, stronger than any relic his father could possess. That The Mother and the Fates existed beyond their prayers. And that they had plans for him and Shaye.

"Sorin!" Bron shouted at him from across the Lake. He held up a fat rabbit and grinned ear-to-ear. The child-like glee on the Mortal Knight's face looked ridiculous when he was practically a giant. He towered over Anik, who stood beside him waving at Ingemar. She waved politely back and pulled her tail from the water. Sorin watched in amazement as the transformation took place before his eyes. Scales slowly disappeared as two legs formed in place of the fin.

"I'll never get used to that." He stood, extending his hand to help her up. She took it, rearranging her nearly sheer gown neatly around her legs. They walked back to the palace together in silence. There was something unspoken between them now. For all the uncertainty of what was still to come, it was comforting to know that he had a band of people, and creatures, that he could rely on. That he could call "friends."

CHAPTER TWENTY-SIX

Shaye

The shades in the room were drawn, allowing the afternoon light to shine through the bedroom window. Her headache had gone away, thanks to Mavka's bittersweet floral tea. Shaye had not even bothered to ask what was in it; by this time she knew better than to question her friend's abilities. *Friend.* It was strange how quickly she had become comfortable with this strange, unlikely crew of Sorin's. She supposed they had been through so much in such a short time, that they had skipped all the awkwardness that came with bringing new people into your life. They had accepted each other, saved, and protected one another.

Sorin's room was like her own, with a four-poster bed. The fire was dying down and she stretched out like a cat. She desperately wanted a bath, so she wandered into the washroom attached to the bedroom. Mavka had drawn her a bath and fetched her a change of clothes.

The water was warm and inviting, filled with oils that had been left behind by the room's former resident. It smelled of roses, and Shaye thought she had never missed the pleasantries of life more than she did in this moment. She dipped her long hair into the water and closed her eyes, trying to remember the missing pieces from the night before. Mavka had assured her that she had nothing to worry about, that it was simply the stress of everything that had been happening.

Bastian had come to sit with her earlier that morning. He did not bring up the night before, and she had been too embarrassed to ask. So, she found herself content to just sit with him, reminiscing about their childhood. They talked of the grand adventures they had gone on in the Raven Wood, of the hot summer days they had spent swimming in the lake, and how they had hidden from the Master Mage whenever he had a test planned for the class.

She had enjoyed their time together, and couldn't help but think of what things would have been like if there had been no uprising. Would she have grown into a poised woman of court? It was hard to imagine the life that could have been if she and Bastian had not been separated. She plunged her head under the water and tried to focus instead, on what the day would hold. Keeping her mind in the present would be crucial if she was to stay focused and keep her friends safe.

Lunchtime was approaching, and Shaye felt well enough now to join the others downstairs. She dressed in the soft dress Mavka had brought her and tied her hair up in a blue silk ribbon, the color of Sorin's eyes. She liked the way the color contrasted in her autumn-colored hair.

Shaye ventured downstairs, feeling refreshed and ready to face the rest of the day. What she found when she entered the parlor made her heart warm. Bron and Sorin were play-fighting using toy swords they had found in one of the rooms. She looked over to Mavka, who was quizzing an extremely uncomfortable Anik about the wonders of women's stockings. She had forgone her vine-layered clothing for a dress like Shaye's and had hiked it up to her thighs to show Anik the ribboned stockings underneath. He shifted in his seat trying to explain to her that a lady should keep her undergarments to herself.

Bastian sat alone in a corner eating from a bowl of freshly picked berries, and smiled at her when she entered. She took the seat beside him, grabbing a handful of berries for herself. Her face puckered at the tartness of them. Even here at the palace, the blight prevented food from growing right.

From the corner of her eye, she noticed a straight-backed Ingemar eyeing her and Bastian from the couch. There was a book in her hands, although it seemed she had no interest in reading it.

"Glad to see everyone getting along down here," Shaye teased, looking pointedly at Bron, who had now abandoned the wooden sword to put Sorin in a headlock. The boys laughed and stepped back from one another.

Bron joked, "Gotta stay spry if we want to protect you, milady." He swept a mocking bow in her direction.

Shaye laughed and stood, walking over to him, the perfect picture of innocence. She put a hand to her heart and curtseyed to the towering knight. Everyone in the room fell into a fit of laughter as Shaye ducked and swept out her leg, knocking the unsuspecting knight off his feet. She grabbed the forgotten toy sword and held it, poised to his throat.

"Yes, we wouldn't want *me* vulnerable to attack, *Sir Bronimir*." She winked and offered a hand to help him up.

He took it, having the good sense to look impressed. She knew he was genuinely surprised. Most people were when they witnessed her in a fight. She had always been curvier, even when she was young, never petite like Mavka. But she had learned the hard way to hold her own. Living with smugglers had tested her endurance, taught her to use the element of surprise. It may have taken a few brawls and a lot of sparring with the other sailors, but she had perfected the art of using their underestimation of her to her advantage.

Sorin and the others cheered and clapped for her, impressed by the performance. She made a show of bowing graciously before they all sat down to eat their lunch of rabbit, berries, and nuts. It was almost enjoyable, being here with this strange group of theirs, eating and joking together. Each one of them was so different, in ability and background, yet here they were, working together for a common goal.

As their meal came to an end, Sorin got that serious look on his face, the one he got when he seemed to remember that he was indeed *king* of this country. It was hard for Shaye to imagine him there at the Summer Palace, performing his kingly duties, dressed in the ridiculous garb of royalty. She preferred him this way, just Sorin, the pain in her ass who was dragging her along on an adventure.

"I've been thinking." He popped a handful of berries into his mouth.

"A dangerous thing," Bron joked.

"Don't I know it." Sorin chuckled and shook his head. "The reality is, we all came here thinking we'd fix the Stave and get out. That it would be a piece of cake and I would have you home in time for the Summer Solstice celebration. I did not anticipate something bigger happening here and I have no right to request anything more from you. If you need to go back, then I understand; you've all played a huge role in getting us to this point and I appreciate it more than you know."

Bron was quick to speak up, "I'm with you, brother. Until the end."

"Me too!" Mavka raised her hand and wiggled around in her seat, sending her moths fluttering around in a frenzy. She looked at Bron and blushed.

Ingemar was the next to pledge, "As I have stated many

times, I will see this through with you. Once the Nefari are defeated, I will go home."

Anik pounded a fist on the table and nodded, "You already know where I stand."

"I appreciate that, Anik. Though, I have something else in mind for you. I will need you to ride back for reinforcements. We need General Tyrell to organize the first army for battle. There is no way to tell yet how big or organized the Nefari forces are, but we need to be ready for anything. I need you to pass on my official orders as King, to have them stationed in the small hunting village we passed just before we hit the lake. The sooner you leave, the better."

Anik pushed his empty plate aside, stood, and saluted, before taking his leave to pack provisions for the ride ahead. All eyes were on Shaye now as they waited for her to give her answer.

"Shaye, I'm sorry I brought you all this way. We thought bringing a Druid descendant to fix the relic would be enough to put things right. But considering we do not even know where the other piece is or what the Nefari have planned... No one would blame you for going back. Anik can escort you—"

"No. Like I told you before, I've come this far. If it's alright, I would like to see it through." The look of relief on Sorin's face did not go unnoticed by Shaye when she answered. The others seemed to make note of it, too, as Bron raised his brows at the exchange.

Bastian chimed in now, "I would like to stay as well." Respectfully, he bowed his head toward Sorin, "That is, if it's alright with you, King Sorin."

A shadow passed over Sorin's face, but still he said, "Of course. We're in no position to turn down help." Sorin turned to Mavka, "Could you find out where these bastards have made their camp? They have gone undetected so they may be using magic to mask their position. If anyone can figure it out, I believe it would be you."

Mavka's head bobbed up and down and she smiled brightly at the compliment. She whispered something and then her moths fluttered away. Off to find answers for them. Shaye felt a tinge of jealousy towards Mavka's ability to use her magic so effortlessly. Perhaps in another lifetime Shaye would have been raised in an environment where her Druid gifts were nurtured, instead of forgotten. Even now, with the power of the Stave broken, she had only been able to really call on the full strength of her powers once.

With everything that had been happening, she had not even had time to practice the basic spells in the book that Sorin had given her. "If I am not needed right now, I would like to spend more time training while we wait for word on the Nefari location. If things get ugly, I need to be able to access my magic."

"Take as much time to train as you'd like. In the meantime, Bron and I will talk about our strategy for after the camp is located. Ingemar, we would welcome any input you may have."

As everyone went off to take care of their respective tasks at hand, Bastian hung back. Shaye was glad he had offered to stay and help. There was so much more she wanted to ask him. Who else had survived and escaped with him? What was it like for them in Skag, and had they faced the same prejudices the Magi faced here in Asterion? More importantly, why hadn't they come back sooner?

"I can help you, you know." He was suddenly remarkably close to her and reached out a hand, touching her arm lightly. He was dressed in a fresh linen shirt and tailor-made breeches that he must have found in one of the guest rooms, but he wore the same boots and black leather gloves that he had arrived in. She put a hand on his.

"Training together would feel like the old days, wouldn't it? When it was just the two of us." He was looking intently into her eyes.

"But without the audience of angry old Mages breathing down our necks." She tilted her head to the side, in awe of the man he had become. She decided to accept his offer. "That sounds wonderful." They moved closer together, and she felt a stirring deep within her, like a flame begging for release.

She closed her eyes and Bastian whispered in her ear, "Don't try so hard, allow your body to relax, feel the magic buried within you, like the very breath in your lungs. Release it." Shaye focused on his words, took a breath and released it slowly. Bastian kissed her; she was surprised by it. She did not lean into the kiss as she had with Sorin, but she stayed still as he pulled back and said, "Open your eyes."

When she did, the room was ablaze with candlelight. Every candle inside the room flickered, casting light shadows in the afternoon shade. "This was me?"

"Shaye, you are capable of so much more than you think. You need to trust me and trust yourself. You'll be more powerful than anyone could ever have imagined."

The pulse of magic still coursed through her. For the rest of the day her and Bastian practiced the simple arts. They excused themselves to the gardens so she could safely wield her magic: wind, fire, water, and earth. Shaye was exhausted, but by dinnertime she had been able to move each element with little to no effort.

Bastian had taken time to explain to her that Druids, unlike Sorcerers, drew their magic directly from nature. It was why enchantments and alchemy had always been a challenge for her. While Sorcerers and Mages had to practice in the Academy to perfect their arts, Druids could perform divine magic as simply as eating or sleeping. Natural magic was a part of her and her bloodline. It was as if she was an extension of Asterion itself.

"Let's take a break," Bastian offered after she had mastered moving the vines in a nearby tree. She was sweating from the strain of picking up large rocks with them like the trees had done with the Naga at Mavka's request.

They sat together and she ran her hands in the hard, brown grass. Bastian moved closer to her. "It's a shame, isn't it?"

"Yes, this was always the most beautiful place in all of Asterion. It's heartbreaking to see it in such a sad state."

"It won't last. We'll restore it to its true beauty." He moved her hair from the nape of her neck, his breath tickling her ear. "Though it will pale in comparison to you. It always has."

Shaye raised a brow. "Bastian, if I didn't know any better, I would say you're flirting with me."

"Would it be so horrible if I was?"

Shaye thought for a moment. There was a time when they were younger that she'd thought he was the most fascinating person in the world. Before they had been separated she had started to notice him more and more as a handsome young man. Now here he was, charming and intriguing.

Turning to him, she found he was close enough to kiss. He leaned in, his lips pressing hard to hers, but the memory of Sorin in the library interrupted her thoughts. This didn't feel right; she pulled back quickly. "Bastian, I..."

He sat back in annoyance, then brushed it off, smiling sweetly at her. He was calm and collected as he dusted off his shirt. "It's okay, I understand; it's too soon."

Shaye wanted to say it was more than that, that something had been slowly blossoming between her and Sorin, something she did not understand and wasn't quite ready to voice out loud; but before the words could touch her lips, she suddenly felt very heavy.

Her thoughts clouded again, making her forget what she had been about to say. She needed rest after exerting herself in the warmth of the day.

"You're tired. Maybe we should call it a day." Bastian offered his arm to her.

Shaking her head to clear her thoughts, she conceded and took his arm. "I could probably use a bite to eat."

She gripped his arm as they walked back to the palace in silence.

CHAPTER TWENTY-SEVEN

Sorin

Sorin sat at the dining table feeling anxious. He wanted to pretend that he was feeling this way because of the stressful afternoon he'd spent trying to come up with a plan, when they knew next to nothing about their enemy. But if he was being honest with himself, he was anxious because Shaye had spent almost the entire day training in the yard with Bastian.

His gut told him that Bastian could not be trusted, while Bron, Mavka, and Anik had told him to trust Shaye. Bron pointed out that his feelings for Shaye were perhaps clouding his judgment. Sorin ultimately agreed in attempt to put everyone at ease while they strategized. There were other matters at hand to focus on and he didn't want to distract them with his own petty problems.

Anik had been eager to get on the road, so he took his leave and Sorin prayed he would make it there in time. More than that, he prayed that Anik would not run into trouble on the road.

Sorin and the others had just sat down to eat when Shaye

entered the room with Bastian. Sorin couldn't help but notice the joy on her face. She was glowing, her eyes even brighter than usual. He did not realize he was staring until Bron elbowed him in the side.

Shaye sat down across from him, launching into updates from her day... How she had tapped into her magic, calling it up as easily as breathing. She held out her hand, fingers twirling above the decanter of water in front of her. Droplets began to rise out of the glass, swirling in the air like rain falling up instead of down. It was incredible. The room erupted in congratulations and praise.

Sorin eyed Bastian. He could not stand the way he looked at Shaye. He looked like a beast eyeing prey right before an attack. Sorin could not hold back anymore, his questions were eating away at them and as much as he wanted to brush it under the rug, he couldn't.

"Bastian, I understand that you've been in Skag. They have zero tolerance for Magi there, if I remember correctly. Was it difficult living under their rule?"

"My friends and I found a quiet village in the northern mountains. It was an adjustment, but we survived."

"And, uh, what did your *friends* think of you coming all this way on your own? They don't share the same sentiments for home as you do?"

Bastian remained cool and collected but Sorin did not miss the aggravation on his face. Bastian quickly replaced it with a look of sincere hurt, before he answered again, "No. They did not feel the same call to come home as I did."

"Sailing through the western sea would be nearly impossible alone; it's often been described as a perilous journey through rocky waters. How did you cross so quickly? Not to mention, word of the broken relic couldn't have hit Skagan shores more than a few weeks ago." Sorin shrugged, attempting to keep a casual air about him. He just needed

Bastian to slip up once. For one small detail to be out of place.

Shaye cut in, "Sorin, what are you doing?"

"Just trying to get to know our newest team member."

"Well, it's starting to sound an awful lot like an interrogation."

Sorin threw his hands up in defense. "Bastian has nothing to hide, isn't that right?"

Shaye pushed her plate aside. "Could we speak? *Privately,* please."

Before he could answer, she shoved her chair back and stormed from the room. He followed her quickly through the kitchens and out into the barnyard. The horses whinnied in surprise at their sudden appearance. The door slammed shut behind them and Shaye spun around, turning on him before he had a chance to speak.

"What are you doing? Bastian has done nothing but try to help since he got here. Just because he's Magi doesn't mean he's Nefari."

"No, it doesn't, but the fact that he shows up here, *alone*, out of the blue, means we should be careful. Even Ingemar cannot get a read on him. *Something* is clearly off and you're too blinded by your past to see it."

"How would you know what I'm too blind to see? Here I am, with you, the son of my people's enemy. I betray the memory of my people, my *family*, by helping *you*."

"Your decision to come with me was entirely your own. I have been honest with you every step of the way. For Mother's sake, I spilled my guts to you last night, told you things I have never spoken of, and you act as if it means *nothing*. Instead, you spend the day with *him*." Sorin wasn't sure why he had said that. He was trying to reason with her, but instead he was sounding like a jealous lover.

"Is that what this is about Sorin? That I'm giving him my

attention?" She stepped closer to him. "Bastian is my oldest friend. He is Magi, like me, and he understands what I am feeling. You are right, I chose to help you and I do not regret that, not for one minute. But today he gave me a gift; he helped me unlock my magic. Please believe me when I say that he is only here to help us." She put a hand to his chest, lingering over his heart. She hesitated before stepping closer to him.

He looked down into her face, searching for what she was really feeling. She spoke again. "I belong to no one in this world. Do not misunderstand, Sorin, I care for you. I care for all of you, but I am *done* feeling afraid. If Bastian can help me get past the fear and tap into my full magic, then it benefits *all* of us. Of all the people in this world, I need *you* to trust me. Please."

Sorin knew pushing her any more on the subject would only make her retreat further into Bastian's influence. He was going to have to *show* her. He had an impulse to touch her cheek but held back. They had not talked about that night in the library, but the memory hung in the air between them. Things had shifted since then, and he was not sure they could go back.

"I *do* trust you Shaye. I trust you with my life. We just have to be careful, to keep all of us safe."

She nodded in agreement and just as quickly as her body had pressed against his, it was gone. She retreated into the house, leaving him with the lingering feeling of something lost.

He kicked a nearby bucket in frustration. The sooner they found the Nefari stronghold, the better. Tomorrow he would scout with Mavka and Bron. Sorin decided to check in on the horses while he was out here. He picked up a pail, filled it with water, and headed to the barn. The horses were pawing at the ground when he entered the dark stables. He searched for a torch and lit it, casting long shadows along the old stone walls. The stables had held up well against the test of time. King Idor had loved horses and had spent more on building the stables than he'd spent on his servants' quarters.

Finn was snorting and thumping against the stall door in a panic. Sorin reached out to calm him, rubbing the horse's neck and whispering soothing words to him. A noise sounded from one of the dark corners of the barn and Sorin realized they weren't alone. He turned to see a massive, black, wolf-like dog, shrouded in shadows. They rolled around its body and Sorin's heart sank when he saw its eyes; they were as red as the gates of hell. It was a Black Shuck, a hellhound.

The hideous dog lunged for Sorin, giving him no time to call out to the others. He waved the fire-lit torch at the beast, pushing it back away from the barn and the horses. It snarled at him, snapping its razor-sharp teeth. Its body wavered; it was as if its very being was unable to hold its form in the light. Black Shucks were uncommon, but he had read reports dating back through the ages. They came from The Beyond, conjured from the shadows to do their master's bidding. Only black magic could create something so perverse. Dread set in as he realized there was no way he was going to outrun it.

Sorin grabbed a nearby pitchfork, all he had to do was keep a safe distance between him and the creature until he could get to his sword. The Black Shuck backed away from him, never taking his eyes from Sorin's throat. It occurred to Sorin that if the hound was here then it's master would be nearby. He had to warn the others if there was an attack coming.

By now, Sorin had turned them around, and he was closer to the door than the hound was. Backing up slowly, he waited until he was a few feet away before he catapulted the pitch-fork at the monstrous canine. The Black Shuck caught the wooded handle in its mouth and snapped it in half. Foam was dripping from its mouth as it poised to pounce. Sorin bolted for the house, before the creature had time to strike, and locked the door behind him.

The Black Shuck threw its monstrous frame against the door, relentless. Sorin could hear it snarling as it tried to break down the only thing standing between it and its prey. Sorin shouted for help, and the group came running to his aid. "Bron! There might be more surrounding the house. Secure the doors and windows. The rest of you, now would be a good time to wield those magical powers of yours!" The door was shaking on its hinges as Sorin pressed his body against it in case it gave in.

Mavka whispered to her moths, and they fluttered off in a blur of gray. Ingemar held out her hands, a glowing gold dust rising from them. "Open the door, King Sorin!" she shouted, the cloud of dust growing bigger. He did as she said. The door launched open just as Ingemar released her magic.

The Black Shuck was knocked across the dirt, landing roughly near the stables. Its matted black fur rose on its back. Razor-sharp teeth snapped in anger. The growl that sounded from the beast was like thunder from a storm. It was already trying to rise when she began to form another cloud, but Shaye stepped in instead. She sent a gust of wind into the dog, knocking it over again, sending it rolling through the dirt and gravel. A silver dust glittered in the wake of her magic, and she gave him a triumphant smile. No anger lingered from their fight before.

It fell onto a tree root and, before anyone could call on their magic again, a vine swept the beast up, launching him out of sight. Jaws dropped open as they turned to Mavka. "That was your doing, I suppose?" Sorin asked, as he pointed to the tree. All they got in response was a shy giggle from the tiny girl.

Bron returned with news that the perimeter was secure. If

its master had been near, then he or she was long gone by now. Bron and the girls retreated into the safety of the palace, but Sorin waited as Shaye went to calm the horses. It was just him and Bastian then. Even in the dark of the night, Sorin could see how pale he had become in all the commotion.

"You alright there, Bastian?"

"Just a lot to process, that's all." He straightened up and smiled confidently as he spotted Shaye returning from the stable. "Shall we end the night with a drink, celebrate a job well done?"

She took the arm he extended to her. "Yes, *please*." She turned to Sorin, "Will you join us?"

As much as he wanted to be with Shaye, he could not bring himself to be around Bastian any more than was necessary. "Not tonight, I'm going to wait a bit, see if the beast returns; but I'll see you in the morning."

Her face fell and she bit her lip, but she said nothing. Sorin watched as they disappeared alone into the house, arm in arm.

Frustration overtook him. Between Bastian and beastly attacks, he needed a win. They would find that damned camp no matter what the cost, he decided. *Tomorrow, we turn the tides.*

CHAPTER TWENTY-EIGHT

Shaye

Shaye *strapped her jeweled* dagger to her thigh. She shrugged on a delicately embroidered jerkin and fitted trousers; they fit her well considering they had probably been made for a small-framed man. Women in the Winter Palace would never have been caught wearing men's clothing, but she didn't care. She had always been more comfortable this way. Besides, her travel clothes were a wreck from the cave incident, and she could not very well wear a dress to hunt down rogue Magi.

She and Bastian had stayed up well into the night. He had always been a dreamer, full of ideals, and he had shared with her all the changes he thought would benefit Asterion. He wanted Magi to regain their powers, to play more of a role in the King's court; not as they once had, but as equals to the humans who now ruled it.

It made sense; it was not anything she had not thought before. Again, she found herself wondering what it would have been like if they had not been separated. Would they have continued to rely on each other, or would they have grown apart as childhood friends often did? They had been deep in the bottle when she finally excused herself to bed.

That night she dreamed of a ballroom, only this time it was not one flowing with blood. It was a beautiful party, and Bastian had twirled her on the dance floor. She found herself in a gown of black, entwined with a beautiful, beaded bodice; it was like magic had been sewn into the very fabric of it. Bastian wore a jacket that matched, like they had been made as a set.

This time, when he had taken her hand and pulled her into that stairwell, it had been to steal away a kiss. He tangled his hands in her hair and kissed her deeply, and she had savored every second. His hands had found their way lower, rounding her breasts and pulling at the beaded bodice.

She had melted into him, wanting more, *needing* more. She moaned his name and lost herself in him. His hands were at her skirts now, pulling them up above her silken stockings. *Shaye*, he purred into her ear, sending lightning currents through her entire body. She savored the way her name sounded on his tongue. Then, just when she thought she would let him take her right there, she awoke.

The dream had felt so real, she could still feel his hands on her body as she washed and dressed for the day. She had to shake this feeling. Sorin needed her head in the right place for this mission. *Sorin. By The Mother, what will I do?* She could not deny there had been something between the two of them before Bastian had shown up. She had come to trust and care for him more than she had thought possible. But now with Bastian here, she couldn't think straight.

When she came downstairs, the others were ready and waiting for her. She blushed when she saw Bastian and had trouble meeting Sorin's eye. "Let's do this."

They made their way toward the forest, Mavka leading the way. Her sources in the Raven Wood had told her that there was dangerous activity to the north of the forest. It took them hours to follow the tree line around, hoping to avoid run-ins with any dangerous creatures lurking in the shadows.

Dusk was nearing as they came to a desolate piece of land. It looked as if it had been scorched by fire, and the smell of sulfur filled the air. Mavka touched the ground, letting the ashy dirt slip through her fingers. "We're close. Their black magic is seeping into the land. The worse the condition of it, the closer we are to them."

They continued further, until they came to an abandoned camp. It looked as if whoever had been there had left in a hurry. Smoke still billowed from the fires around the encampment, and supplies were strewn around carelessly. Shaye and the others ventured further into the camp, on high alert for anyone who may have stayed behind.

"King Sorin, you need to see this." Ingemar was standing by a large pillar that had been buried into the ground. As Shaye followed Sorin to the pillar, she could see that it was sloppy work, tilted to the side as if it would give at any moment and topple over. The smell of rotting flesh was almost unbearable, the closer she came.

When she stepped close enough for a clear view, Shaye gasped at the horror in front of them. A man was strung up; he had been there for a while by the look and smell of him. Except as they came closer, Shaye realized he was not human. His skin was a soft green like Mavka's. Curved horns sprouted proudly from his head, common amongst male Forest Dwellers.

A crow sat perched atop the pillar. He cawed wildly at the sight of them. Mavka let out a wail and dropped to her knees when she saw the Dweller hanging. Bron was by her side in an instant, cradling her in his large arms. Shaye tried to hold back the vomit rising in her at the horrid sight. She wanted to go to her friend, to help Bron comfort her, but she couldn't move. She could not bring herself to do anything but stand there, rooted to the putrid ground that was tainted with black magic and the death of one of its own.

Sorin took the Forest Dweller down from the post, cutting the ties that held the poor creature's hands above his head, his limp body nearly knocking Sorin into the ground. He laid him down gently, saying a quiet prayer over him. Mavka knelt, whispering what Shaye guessed were the resting rites of her people. Mavka dragged branches to his body, placing them neatly over him, and closed his eyes in respect.

"From the land you are born and to the land you return." Mavka bowed her head and put a hand to her heart.

Shaye accompanied Sorin and the others to search the camp, looking for any sign of where the Nefari might be headed next. It was strange to see how mundane each tent was. There were no signs of the darkness that resided within its former tenants. Cups were left half full, papers were strewn around, signs that they had left in a hurry. Shaye sifted through the papers; there was nothing significant in any of them. She huffed in frustration, "There's nothing useful here."

"Take them anyways, we'll look through them again later, see if we missed anything." Sorin took them from her so he could tuck them into his pack.

"King Sorin!" Ingemar shouted from outside of the tent.

They ran out just in time to see a hooded figure retreating into the forest. Before he could get lost in the tree line, Bron appeared, throwing out a muscled arm and knocking the Magi to the ground. He held out his sword before the man could move away.

Shaye and the others caught up to them. Mavka was standing beside Bron, bouncing on her feet. "I want to kick him."

Bron put a hand on Mavka's shoulder to steady her. "I know... but we typically refrain from that sort of thing."

The man spat at Bron's feet and Bron rolled his eyes. "On second thought, maybe I *should* let her kick you."

The man raised his hands to call on his magic; the very tips of his fingers were black. He was Nefari. Ingemar blocked the magic with her own and the Nefari looked up at them with a snarl, "Do what you want with me, it doesn't matter anymore, you're too late to save them." His laugh sent chills down Shaye's spine.

Bron growled, "Oh, we're not going to kill you." He pulled the Nefari from where he laid on the ground. "We have other plans for you." He dragged the Magi into one of the tents. The Nefari cursed at him under his breath.

"Wait. You're going to torture him?" Bastian said before he began to follow Bron and their captive to the tent.

Sorin blocked his path. "We're going to do what's necessary to find out what he knows. But I assure you, Bron will ask before he acts."

Bastian turned to Shaye, panic on his face. Shaye shook her head at him, "I trust Sorin to do what needs to be done. We don't have the luxury, or the time, to spare him."

"So, you would condone the torture of your own kind?" Bastian was pleading with her now.

"He is not *our* kind, Bass. You see what they did to that innocent creature. We need to stop them." She didn't like how this was all playing out, but she felt like they were running out of options, and she trusted both Bron and Sorin to do what they could *before* resorting to more violent means.

Bastian went to her; Sorin shifted on his feet as if he would stop him but stayed where he was. Shaye allowed Bastian to take her hands in his. "Shaye, listen to me."

Sorin cut in, pushing between her and Bastian. "No. Bastian, you listen to *me*. You have no authority here."

Shaye was feeling lightheaded and needed a moment to

think. She spoke, "Bastian, please excuse us. I would like to speak to Sorin alone."

Bastian did as she asked, storming away, and disappearing behind one of the tents. Mavka and Ingemar silently excused themselves as well, lingering out of earshot by the forest line.

"Sorin, are you sure this is the only way?"

He looked down at his feet. She could sense that he did not feel right about what he was about to do. "I don't see another way, do you?"

"I don't know. I'm just so tired." Another headache was coming on again and she felt like she should sit down.

Before they could say anything else, a blast came from the tent where Bron had been holding the prisoner. Shaye and Sorin ducked in surprise as a plume of smoke rose from where the tent had once been. Bron was thrown, hitting the ground with a thud.

He rose slowly, appearing to be unharmed. When the dust settled, they saw the Nefari they had captured, laying in the debris from the blast. A knife had been plunged into his heart and he laid in a pool of his own blood, staring up to the sky with blank eyes.

"What the hell?" Bron swore as he ran to the Nefari to see if he was still breathing. He shook his head; their only lead was dead. "He was confined one minute and the next, something hit. Sorin, I swear to you I didn't see his hands move; he wielded no magic. It came from somewhere else." Bron looked around wildly. "Where did he even get the bloody dagger?"

"Where is Bastian?" Sorin demanded.

"You think Bastian is responsible for this? Are you insane?" Shaye was appalled at the accusation. "Only moments ago, he had been pleading on the man's behalf, why would he kill him after something like that?"

"Moments ago he was trying to stop us. Now our only lead

to the Nefari whereabouts is laying there *dead*." Sorin was mad with rage.

"He did this to *himself*, Sorin." She needed to get a grip on the situation, emotions were running too high. "You're jealous and you're not thinking clearly."

"*I'm* not thinking clearly?" Sorin was visibly shaking now. Shaye could not understand why he was passing blame onto Bastian. His face turned red with furry. "Since he has arrived, things have only gotten worse. He's hiding something and everyone can see it but *you*."

Shaye backed away, anger fueling her. "Enough! You are so far in over your head that you're finding fault in him where there is none." Darkness was beginning to cloud her vision and she put a hand to her head.

"Shaye, *listen to me*." Sorin begged her.

"No, you listen to me. I have given up everything to follow you here, put my grievances with your family aside, and now you accuse my friend of working with the enemy... Accuse him of *murder*."

"You need to set those feelings aside and see what is right in front of your eyes!" They were shouting at each other now.

"You know what, *Your Majesty*, you drive me crazy." She turned to walk away from him; She needed to sit down, to catch her breath.

"Well, that doesn't take much, does it!" He shouted at her back as she walked away.

"What's going on here?" Bastian reappeared in front of Shaye, looking bewildered. He went to her side, steadying her as she stumbled toward a nearby stump.

Sorin looked murderous. He turned on Bastian. "Do you know anything about this?" He pointed to the dead forest creature whose heart had been carved from his chest. Then to the Nefari, still laying in a dark pool of his own blood. "Tell the truth Bastian, have you ever seen this creature or this man before today?"

Bastian looked shocked at the accusation. "Of course not. I *told* you, I came *alone* from the West." He left Shaye alone on the stump and strode back toward Sorin.

Sorin struck him in the face, throwing him into the dead earth. He was on him in seconds. Shaye yelled out to him, but there was no stopping him. He tore into Bastian like a wild animal. Shaye closed her eyes; summoning her magic, she called on the ground to tremble, but nothing came. The land here had nothing left to give her. So, she did the next thing she could think of and threw herself into Sorin, tumbling to the ground with him. Bastian scrambled to stand, dusting himself off and wiping the blood from his face with the back of his sleeve.

He had a rabid look in his eyes as he yelled at Sorin, "You *dare* accuse *me* of betrayal? *King* Sorin, maybe we should count *your* sins instead of *mine*." Sorin looked at him in confusion, still on the ground, next to Shaye. They both paused to hear what Bastian had to say.

Bastian went to Shaye, kneeling before her. "My only sin is not telling you sooner."

"Telling me what, Bastian?"

"Of how your parents met their fate." His eyes bore into hers and he spoke with a deep sense of urgency. "The usurper, King Allerick, ordered an attack on the last of the Druid bloodline. He knew it was they who protected the relics, the only ones who knew where to find them. He sent his people to take the Stave and ordered them to leave no survivors."

Sorin looked like he could spit venom. He gritted between his teeth, "*Liar.*"

Clouds began to darken the sky and a chill filled the air. Bastian inched closer to Shaye; he looked intently in her eyes. His gaze felt like fire in her soul. "I'm telling you the truth. His father was a cold-blooded murderer and so is he." He pointed to Sorin, who was standing now, speechless.

"Sorin would have you become a slave to him. Only allowing you your power so long as you do *his* bidding. Have you forgotten your own people Shaye? They need you now more than ever. Only you can control and guard the relics. Without you we will remain stagnant in this life, doomed to wither away in a mediocre existence."

Shaye could not take her eyes from him. Everything around her went silent, even the cawing of the crow high above them. Bastian would not lie to her. He loved her, had always loved her. It had been the two of them since the beginning. Sorin barely knew her; he claimed to need her, but for what? So she could help him destroy magic as his father had done?

Images flashed in her mind. Her mother was telling her to run, to look for her aunt and uncle in the palace. She saw a village, not far from where they were now, filled with slaughtered Druids, strung up for the crows to feast on. The smell of fire filled her nose, and she could feel the seeds of fear that had been planted in her at that moment.

Her mind went foggy again, and all she could feel was the growing need for vengeance. *Blood for blood.* She would make them pay for everything they had done to her people, to her parents, to her. Fire rose from within her, not from the land but from someplace else; somewhere far darker. And colder.

She could hear distant shouting, but she could not recognize the voices anymore; she no longer cared. She felt like she would be consumed by the hate that was filling her. She needed to release it, to make the world *feel* it. *Let go,* a voice whispered from within her. She did as the voice bid. Fire exploded from her, knocking her back into the darkness.

CHAPTER TWENTY-NINE

Sorin

A fter the blast, *Sorin* regained consciousness, but it was too late. Bastian was gone, and with him, Shaye. He hit the rough ground with a curse. How could he have risked them like that? Everything in him had screamed not to trust that bastard, but he had been so afraid of losing Shaye. He had lost her in the end, anyway.

Panic coursed through him as he looked around for the others. Bron had shielded Mavka with his body, his armor protecting them both. Ingemar had lifted a shield between her and the blast, keeping the brunt of the force off her.

Anger burned in her eyes. "I should have seen this coming."

Sorin dusted himself off, limping over to her. "It's not your fault. I knew he could not be trusted. I thought by allowing him to come today, by keeping him close, he would slip up and somehow give himself away."

"He gave himself away alright. A damned Nefari, sleeping and eating with us for *days*," Bron growled from where he and Mavka stood. He held tight to her as she clung to him with a tear-streaked face.

Sorin ran a hand through his hair. "She's gone."

"So is the Stave." Bron pointed to Sorin's pack a few feet away. It had been thrown in the blast from Shaye.

Ingemar hissed, reminding him of the sea creature lurking within the beautiful woman. "He's not just any Nefari. I recognized what he was doing the moment he started talking. I tried to extend my magic toward him, to stop him, but his shields were too strong."

"What do you mean, not just any Nefari?"

"I mean he's incredibly powerful. To be able to block my magic while getting inside of her head would take a great deal of strength. It takes dark, blood magic to be able to control another's thoughts and memories like that."

Mavka spoke, "He is a Shadow Dancer. A son of Obsidian. I recognized it, too, the way he swayed Shaye so easily with his words."

Her memories. How could he have been so blind. Shaye had been acting strange since the moment Bastian had arrived. He had thought it was just childhood feelings for him, but that had not explained the memory loss after he had told her about the night of the Winter Solstice ball.

Like a parasite, Bastian had dug his way into her mind, planting doubt in her. All leading up to this moment when he could turn her against Sorin completely. It was despicable. And brilliant. Sorin had failed to protect her, but he would not give up on her so easily.

"By now Anik will have gotten word to the Summer Palace. But it will take them days to reach the village. We can only hope that the Nefari don't reach it first."

Sorin had planned for something like this, for Bastian's betrayal, although that plan had not included a rescue mission for Shaye. He had been sure to announce his plans for his forces to set up their encampment in the hunting village where Bastian could hear. What Bastian had not heard was

Sorin's private instructions for Anik to direct their forces along the eastern coast, sweeping in from behind.

One part of the army would come in from the south, a distraction for the Nefari, and lie in wait at the village, while the other soldiers came in from behind launching an attack on three sides. The only place that would be left for them to run would be to the west, where they would be met with a raging river, and more Asterion troops. He prayed that General Tyrell would get them there in time because there was no way he was going to wait before going after Shaye.

Something throbbed at his side, and he let out a deep groan. His knees hit the ground as he went down from the pain. Mavka and Ingemar rushed to his side, fumbling at his jacket for any sign of what was causing the pain.

Mavka gasped when they revealed the source. There was a deep gash in his side from where the brunt of Shaye's magic had hit him. It wasn't a fatal wound but it had cut him deeply enough that blood was spilling at an alarming rate.

Mavka searched her pack. "We need to get the bleeding to stop."

Ingemar called on her magic and pooled it at the wound. "I should be able to hold it off while you prepare the bandages."

Sorin pushed them away. "No, we need to go. If we hurry, we may be able to catch up to them."

Mavka pushed him back to the ground with more force than he thought she was capable of. "You will be of no use to her, or to any of us, if you are wounded." More softly she added, "We will get her back, King Sorin. You have to believe that."

He shook his head ruefully. "If anything happens to her I'll never forgive myself."

Bron crouched down with them. "None of us will. We all care for her, Sorin. We might be a mess, but we're family." He looked at Mavka when he said the words and smiled.

Sorin shut his eyes tight as Ingemar withdrew her magic, allowing Mavka to tightly bandage the gash. *Family.* Bron was right, after all they had been through they had become more than allies.

Mavka finished tending to him and sat back on the ground, her voice was hushed when she spoke. "Why did he say all of those things, King Sorin?"

He held back a sigh. "I don't know, Mavka. Honestly, I don't."

They sat in silence for a while with the sun fading over the horizon. Sorin felt nothing but despair and pain. The scene with Shaye played over again in his head. She had been so angry with him, so ready to tear the world apart. He knew she struggled with her past, but he never imagined her turning on him like that. Bastian had done a number on her and had defeated them in the process.

He turned toward the unlikely band of heroes. There was no way he was going to let Bastian get the best of them again. They had gotten this far, their lives now intertwined by fate. It was time to dust themselves off and finish this thing once and for all.

He broke the silence. "We're going to need help."

Mavka's head shot up and she smiled, flashing her teeth. "I know just who to ask."

Within moments, Sorin and the others had readied themselves for a journey into the Raven Wood. There was no time to waste. Sorin grabbed the horses, trying to calm Finn. "I know buddy, we'll get her back. I promise." The horse whinnied in response and Sorin saw sorrow in the steed's eyes.

He tied Finn's reins to his own horse's saddle, feeling that same sorrow, and they set off. They were riding into the unknown, but one thing was certain, Sorin would go to the ends of the earth to get Shaye back.

CHAPTER THIRTY

Shaye

When *Shaye awoke*, she found herself in a tent surrounded by lanterns and candlelight. The bed she was on was covered in warm furs and strewn with feather-filled pillows. Confusion washed over her. Her whole body ached, and when she tried to sit up, her chest screamed in pain.

She looked around in awe and confusion at the finery inside of the tent. Lush pillows sat on a chaise lounge by the corner, on top of an elaborate rug. There was a large wooden desk covered in papers and a grand round table in the middle of the tent with a map laid across it. She pushed through the pain and went to the map, looking around for signs of anyone lurking in the shadowy corners as she crossed the space.

The detail on the map was incredible; she recognized it as a map of Asterion that even included shading where the blight had spread. To her horror, she realized it had spread further south, overtaking the southernmost border of Norbrach.

She needed to warn Sorin. She turned to look for him, and

put a hand to her mouth as she remembered the events from earlier in the day. She recalled the argument with Sorin and the look of betrayal on his face as she had listened to Bastian. It was hard to know what to believe anymore. All she knew was that she had lost herself in her anger. A vision of Sorin falling to his knees in the blast sent her stumbling back.

Silent tears ran down her face and she saw her reflection in a tall mirror across the tent; someone had washed her and changed her out of her filthy clothes. She was wearing a sleek black dress now, made of expensive silk. It sparkled in the candlelight, reminding her faintly of the dream she'd had of her and Bastian in the ballroom where they had danced. She touched the smooth fabric that clung to the curves of her body, and when the reflection of her hand caught her eye, she cried out. The tips of her fingers were as black as midnight. *Oh Fates, what have I done?* In her panic she ran for the flaps of the tent's entrance. *Sorin. Where is Sorin?*

The second she stepped out of the tent, she was flanked by two armed guards. They were dressed in sickly green cloaks that shined like oil and they put their hands on the hilts of their swords when they saw her. *Black hands. No. No. No. This isn't happening. He was right. Sorin, I need to get to Sorin.* Her head was spinning and every muscle in her body screamed in pain and exhaustion. There had been a blast... *I was the blast.*

She put her hands to her head, then held them out in front of her, moving them under the dim moonlight. Her fingers were black, and she only knew of one thing that could have caused that. *But I would never do that. I would never hurt them.* She let out a frustrated sob and turned to the men. Through gritted teeth, she demanded, "Bring me to him."

"No need, love." Bastian stood a few feet away, unscathed from her attack in the abandoned camp.

"Explain yourself, you son of a bitch!" She moved on him,

but a force blocked her path. She looked at the guards, who had not moved an inch. But she noticed each had a black hand extended in front of them, they were using their magic to protect him. She would not have the strength to fight them, and insults would get her nowhere. More softly, she pleaded, "Please, Bastian, tell me what happened."

He motioned for the Nefari beside her to lower the magic field and they obeyed immediately. She looked around at the neat rows of tents and the men and women standing outside, watching the heated exchange. A hush had fallen over the camp and Shaye felt panic rising in her.

It was an army; he had organized an army of dark Magi to destroy Asterion. She noticed then that he was holding the Stave. It was in one piece again, no sign that it had ever been split. Its smooth wood stood tall in Bastian's hand, not even a splinter out of place. She had delivered the relic into the hands of their enemy.

"We are not your enemy, Shaye." He spoke out loud, as if he had read her thoughts. Anger rose in her. How dare he bring her here; she needed to find Sorin, to know that he and the others were okay. How had she let her hatred overtake her like that? She had trusted them, known that they were not her enemy, and still she had turned on them.

Bastian approached her. "They're fine. I know you are worried about them. But don't you see? You do not have to hide who you are anymore. Not with me. I know what it's like to not want anyone to see."

She backed a step away from him. "To see what?" Angry tears filled her eyes.

"Through the cracks. We all have them." He gestured to the Nefari surrounding them in the camp. He was inching toward her slowly like she was a wounded animal in the woods, and he was the hungry predator ready to feast.

217

"Yes, I suppose we do. Some a little deeper than others, wouldn't you agree, Bastian?" Defiance was once again growing within her. Her body still ached, but she would fight if she had to.

He chuckled and closed in on her, grabbing her arm and pulling her into the tent roughly. She struggled under his grip. She would not make this easy for him. She would let him know that she was stronger than the little girl he remembered from childhood. And though he was right, she was broken and cracked, she was not beyond repair. She would fix the mess she had made, even if it meant leaving *him* in pieces.

They were alone in the military-styled tent now, but she still sensed the guards outside and knew there was nowhere for her to run. He motioned for her to sit, but she did not obey. Instead, she stood stubbornly, arms crossed and chin raised.

"Shaye, please, I never meant to deceive you. But you weren't ready for the truth." He removed the leather gloves from his hands and Shaye's heart dropped. Black hands, all the way to the wrist. It looked as if someone had poured black ink over them. His fingers were completely black, but as it came closer to his wrist, lines intertwined allowing for a glimpse of pale skin underneath. How had she not noticed it before? She had been so blinded by her need to pick up where they had left off, that she had allowed herself to ignore all the signs.

He poured an amber liquid from the decanter on his desk. A glass for each of them. Shaye looked around the tent for another exit; maybe she could get him drunk and sneak away once he was asleep. As she looked for an escape, a snarl came from behind her.

"I wouldn't do that if I were you. He loves a good chase, and I'm not sure you have enough left in you to run, after what you did back at our old camp."

Shaye turned to find herself standing face to face with the Black Shuck from the stables. He bared his teeth and snapped, as if daring her to make a run for it.

"You're his master. It was *you* who set him loose on Sorin in the stables. Did you have him attack you as well? The night that you came to us?"

Bastian handed her the drink, downing his and then motioning for her to do the same. She drank obediently, still eyeing the canine as it stalked over to Bastian's side. He fed it some meat from a half-eaten plate and ignored her accusation.

"Sorin was right, you're Nefari." She knew she should be surprised but something deep in her gut told her she had always known. "It wasn't exhaustion or stress that was causing my headaches and loss of memory, was it? It was you. How could you do that to me?"

The Black Shuck stalked over to her, saliva dripping from its mouth. She sat then, drink in hand. Bastian whistled at the beast, making him sit on his hind legs in front of her.

"You weren't ready before, but you are now. You see *them* for what they really are: traitors and oppressors. When I realized we had amassed enough power and numbers for an assault, I knew I needed you with me. But I had never imagined you would come to me at the Winter Palace. Destiny has brought us back together, Shaye. It was a gift from The Mother herself. Sure, you resisted more than I had expected. Sending you those dreams wasn't enough to turn you to me, though we did come remarkably close that night in the Raven Wood. I honestly thought you would jump from that cliff and into my grasp."

"That was you in the fog? You manipulated me."

"I apologize for that. But with you, the last of your Druid bloodline, we can wield the relics. I can teach you to combine divine magic with blood magic, making you more powerful

219

than any other in the continent. No one would dare stand against us." His eyes burned into hers and she began to lose her train of thought. She could not think straight with him here.

"Go to hell." She moved to get up, to get away from him, but he knelt before her, planting his black hands firmly on her thighs.

He caressed them as he snarled, "Sweetheart, I *am* hell."

Shaye struggled to gather her thoughts, something had been in that drink... She dropped it to the floor, spilling the last drops of liquid on the intricate rug. Bastian moved closer to her, his mouth lingering in front of hers. "We will rule this wretched country together. Humans and Magi around the world will kneel before us, just as I kneel before you now. Once we hold the remaining relic, we will be unstoppable."

She leaned toward him, her head was spinning... She just wanted it to stop.

"That's right, Shaye, give in to it. Take the power that is yours by birthright. Harness your nightmares and make *the world* feel the fear that you have endured for so long."

As he spoke, something in her mind tugged at her, trying to make her remember. *A boy with deep blue eyes like the sea during a storm.*

"Shaye." Bastian grabbed her chin, making her look at him. "It was *me*. It was always me. Let go of him. *This* is where you belong now." He kissed her; it was not a kiss of longing and love but one of hunger and possession. When he pulled back from her, his eyes were dark; the whites were no longer there, instead it was just an empty pool of black... A reflection of his soul and what the black magic had done to it.

Her heart ached for someone. Someone who had danced with her in a dusty library in the dim light of the moon. Someone who had believed in her. Her mind was growing foggy, and no matter how hard she fought, she could not recall who it had been. Bastian's soothing voice echoed in her mind: *it was a dream. It was all a dream.* And with that, she let go, giving herself into the darkness.

READ ON FOR A SNEAK PEEK OF BOOK
TWO IN THE LEGACY OF DARKNESS
SERIES: A Legacy of Nightmares

CHAPTER ONE

Shaye

The darkness was all consuming. It shrouded Shaye like a warm blanket. She felt safe here, safe from herself and the horror that awaited her on the other side. It had been days since she had succumbed to it, allowing herself to fall into its depths, where pain and guilt could no longer reach her.

Bastian had been right when he had promised the power she would feel if she would just give in to him. There were no nightmares here, no memories to torment her, only strength and the urge to use it. Still, something tugged on her heart and soul, calling her to return. She could not remember why she had been so consumed with helping the son of her enemy, the man who had betrayed her people; why she had let him touch her, kiss her, manipulate his way into her heart.

It was safe here, with Bastian, he would set everything right, she knew that now. King Sorin did not deserve her forgiveness, nor did the people who had taken her magic away. Magi had suffered for too long under a rule that had made them give up a piece of themselves, that part of their souls that cried out to be released.

How could she have let herself become so lost? Shaye was determined to make them pay for what they had done. The Nefari were not her enemy, not anymore. No, she would rise with them, a force more powerful than anything Asterion had ever seen.

By Bastian's side, she would take back her magic, and they would claim what was rightfully theirs. He had only ever wanted to protect her, from the moment they met in the palace as children, when he took a beating for her from that bully. Nobody would ever hurt the two of them again, not if they protected one another.

Shaye, Bastian's voice beckoned her in the darkness, *it is time for you to wake. We have work to do.*

She did as he asked, pushing through the darkness that enveloped her. She opened her eyes. Bastian smiled down at her with his solid black eyes, black like the Obsidian pendant he wore around his neck. The whites of them were gone now. But she was no longer afraid, she felt no anger towards him, and she could not remember why she had ever been angry with him to begin with. He was like a dark prince, *her* dark prince.

He extended a hand to her; their jet-black fingers linking together. Lightening coursed through her as her power answered him. It was time.

ACKNOWLEDGMENTS

I'm still in awe at the fact that I have a book out in the wild. When I began this journey, I never anticipated finding such a welcoming community of authors and readers who wanted to read the stories that have been running amuck inside my head. I am deeply humbled by all the love and support from my readers, friends, and family.

First, to my husband, Zach, who has supported all my whims. You are the most patient and supportive man I have ever met, and I could not have done this without you. From entertaining the kids so I could write uninterrupted, to waiting up for me on late editing nights, and letting me vent when the imposter syndrome kicked in. Thank you, honey, for helping to make a lifelong goal of mine possible.

To my kids. Thank you for bringing me out of my daydreams, for reminding me to enjoy playtime and sunshine. I love you both more than the Northern Lights of Asterion!

To my mom. You have shown me what a strong, female character should look like. You have taught me to grow from the trials in life, and how to persevere. Thank you, for encouraging me to fuel my imagination and for telling me anything is possible.

To my best friend, Catherine... The Brina to my Shaye, who was the first to talk about my story with me like we were in book club! Thank you for inspiring me to write about fierce friendships. (and for letting me use your dad as inspiration for Rolland and his cooking!)

To my family: my dad, stepmom, and grandparents. Thank you for supporting me through all the twists and turns, for never skipping a beat in supporting me when I announced I would be writing my first book.

To my mapmaker, Melissa Nash. Thank you for bringing the world of Asterion, Sagon, and Skag to life. You took my messy sketch and turned it into something tangible. Without you, my readers would still be trying to figure out where Shaye and Sorin were going.

To my betas: Ardena, Catherine, Diana, Lisa, and Stephanie. You were the first people to entrust my characters and world to. Thank you for being the first steppingstone in this process, and for making me smile at your reaction notes as you read!

To my editor, Phoebe Zimmer. Thank you for helping me to see the bigger picture... and all the commas I missed.

To my final editor, Aunt Suzie and her bundle of red pens. Thank you for the corrections, and for the late-night pep talks.

To all of the writers who have come before me. Thank you for shaping my world with your stories and inspiring me to create worlds of my own.

To my readers and fans. Thank you for your support and encouragement through your sweet messages, posts, and reviews. I am immensely thankful for each, and every one of you. It is because of you, that I have the drive to continue sharing these stories with the world. Truly, *thank you.*

ABOUT THE AUTHOR

J.M. Wallace is a proud military wife. She has spent much of her adult life moving from place to place with her husband and their two children, making stories of their own. As a young girl, J.M. was fascinated with stories that she read and that she dreamed up on her own. Even when she was horseback riding, she was never in her own yard; instead, she was in an enchanted forest or riding into battle alongside brave knights. Today, she puts those stories to paper, to share with the world. She does this in the little pockets of her day between giving her kids snacks, naps, baths, and putting them to bed. *A Legacy of Darkness* is her first story.

CONNECT WITH J.M
INSTAGRAM @J.M.WALLACEAUTHOR
TikTok @jmwallace.author